Deadly Island I

by Geoffrey Sleight

I do not know what I may appear to the world, but to myself I seem to have been only like a boy playing on the seashore, and diverting myself in now and then finding a smoother pebble or a prettier shell than ordinary, whilst the great ocean of truth lay all undiscovered before me.

Isaac Newton

CHAPTER 1

THERE are times in life when you wish you could turn back the clock. Reset the moment when you agreed to do something that seemed a good idea at the time, only later to find it was a big mistake.

That's how the episode began after an old friend, Lawrence Keating, rang me one day.

"Alex, how are you keeping? I've bought an island off the west coast of Scotland. Come and spend a few days with me."

Lawrence was the only person I knew who would have enough money to buy an island. We'd met five years earlier at a business college. The fact that we were both aged 22 and shared the same birth date in May had instantly connected us.

He was the flyaway student, brilliant in sales and marketing strategies to the extent his knowledge often exceeded the tutors. But he was modest with it. Friendly, the life and soul of the party. No-one could be envious or annoyed with him.

"You've bought an island? That's amazing." I was impressed, though not surprised Lawrence could do something like that.

"It's not exactly a sun-baked paradise island, but fantastically atmospheric," he said. "There's an old mansion there that needs a lot of renovation, but I've got plans in hand for it. Come and meet me."

As it happened I was between jobs. That is, having recently lost my job as manager of an office equipment store which had gone into liquidation. I wasn't a brilliant student like Lawrence, but the difference in ability didn't stop us from enjoying each other's company at the college.

"Where should I meet you and when?" I asked.

"Why now. No time like the present. I've got a motor launch moored at an old fishing harbour at Tullochrie on the north west coast of Scotland. The island's about five miles offshore there. It's called Fennamore. You might have heard of it."

I hadn't, but then I wasn't an expert on Scottish islands.

"It's a long drive from London. It'll have to be tomorrow," I told him. "I've a few things to sort out."

"All right. Tomorrow. There's a pub by the harbour called the The Ship Inn. I'll meet you there."

"It'll be about two o'clock," I said.

"Okay, but don't be late. See you then." Lawrence hung up.

That was him all over. Driving people to agree to something before they'd hardly had a chance to take it in. That was the secret of his success.

Fortunately his invite had come at the right time. Being between jobs I had a bit of time to spare. There were a couple of interviews lined up, but not for another week. And I hadn't seen Lawrence in over a year. It would be good to meet up again.

My girlfriend, Rosie, was away on a training course from work and wouldn't be back for a few days. She was in sales for a cosmetics company and forging ahead with a

great career. By coincidence, her course was only sixty miles away from the coastal town in Scotland where I'd agreed to meet Lawrence.

It was an eight-hour-drive from my London flat in Fulham and I arrived at Tullochrie just before two o'clock. Lawrence was standing outside The Ship Inn, wearing black chinos and a light blue shirt patterned with yachts and motor boats. The seafaring theme had obviously grabbed him.

His fair hair, blue eyes and square jawline gave him an assertive look that immediately instilled confidence. You could see how this would literally give him a head start in convincing business partners and customers that he was their man.

"Alex, you wonderful person. It's fantastic to see you again," he greeted me with a hug. "Isn't this an amazing place."

I looked around, taking in the colourful boats bobbing gently on the harbour water, seagulls gliding in the breeze, and the rippling sea beyond stretching to the horizon. Grey stone cottages bordered the harbour front and sides, with narrow lanes at each end leading into the small town behind.

"Inspirational isn't it?" Lawrence placed his arm around my shoulders. "So great to see you again."

He was always over the top with everything. But that was his magnetic charm.

"Making loads of money?" he asked.

"Not exactly at this minute," I answered honestly.

"Never mind," he smiled. "I can give you a steer to some amazing investments. Make you rich overnight."

"Great," I replied. "But right now I feel really knackered after a long drive. Can we get something to eat?"

"Sorry, sorry. I'll buy you lunch. Come on."

We entered the pub and after boosting my system with steak pie and chips downed with a beer I felt renewed.

As we made our way along the harbour to where Lawrence's 30-foot, blue and white motor launch Pioneer was berthed, he recited all the technical details about the boat. He'd already filled my head with many of its features over lunch. His enthusiasm was unstoppable.

If only I'd know what was to come, I'd have turned back at that moment and driven home to London. As it was, my horrific future was already unfolding.

Outside the harbour the sea was choppy and the launch bounced furiously over the waves. I wasn't the best seafarer and my stomach began to protest.

Lawrence was in his element.

"Yippee," he yelled, and accelerated causing the craft to whack into the waves even harder.

"Soon be there," he called to me from the wheel, as I sat on the deck enduring the violent impact and feeling like death.

"There's Fennamore island!" he shouted excitedly a short while later. I glanced ahead. The outline of the island was partly covered in a blue-grey mist, giving it a mysterious, almost threatening appearance, as if a warning to stay away.

"I own that," Lawrence announced loudly, bristling with pride as he began turning the launch towards a small inlet. The opening led to a curved pebbly bay with a projecting stone jetty to the side. The bay waters were calmer and with the boat no longer furiously bouncing I began to feel better. Lawrence steered the craft alongside the jetty.

"There's the house," he pointed to a large greystone mansion, which it would be difficult to miss given its size. The steeply pitched slate roof was pitted with extensive patches of moss. A ledge spanned the building just below the roof line with gargoyles perched on each side of the facing corners, fanged teeth and vicious claws projecting into the skyline.

The building loomed at the top of a steep slope overlooking the bay. I felt uncomfortable in its towering presence. The tall, leaded-light front windows seemed to peer curiously like a collection of eyes assessing the new arrival to their island domain.

Lawrence had no such qualms.

"Come on, let's get inside," he called tying the boat ropes to capstans on the jetty. I grabbed my overnight bag and followed.

We walked up the steep gravel track dividing a wide grass slope rising to the house. The view on each side as we neared the top opened across fields and a distant spread of pine trees to the right shrouded in mist.

Crunching yet more gravel underfoot across the broad forecourt at the top, we reached a short flight of steps taking us to the stately oak door entrance.

"Isn't it amazing," Lawrence continued to enthuse.

"Yes," I agreed, "but you've definitely got your work cut out."

As we grew closer to the building I could see much of the stonework was eroding with age and neglect, cracks in places and the wood frames on many of the windows rotting.

"I've got great plans for this place," Lawrence's spirit was undeterred. "Just needs money and a lot of TLC. The last owner Lord Ernest Loftbury died broke. The place had been falling apart for years. That's how I got the island and house for a knock down price. No-one could see its potential like me."

The oak front door began to open. An elderly man in a white, open neck shirt and grey trousers appeared. There was no sign of welcome on his grizzled face, merely an unemotional stare.

"This is Andrew McKellan, my butler, caretaker and general maintenance man," Lawrence introduced him. "And this is our guest, Alex Preston, a good friend of mine from college days," he announced, slapping me on the shoulder.

The man just nodded acknowledgement of my presence and held out his hand to take my travel bag.

"Andrew will drop that in your room and his wife, Laura, will bring us some coffee and cakes in the sitting room." Lawrence beckoned me inside as his employee disappeared inside with my bag.

The entrance hall was huge. A vast candelabra hung above the setting, attached to a chain stretching two-storeys up to the roof. Dark wood panelling filled the expanse, with a wide stairway to the right sweeping up to balconies over-looking the hall on the first and second floors.

It was a grand setting, but now tarnished with age. Many of the glass beads in the candelabra were missing and the remainder coated in dust. The panelling and several doors off the hallway looked faded and scuffed.

Within moments of us entering an elderly, grey-haired woman emerged from a side passage at the back of the hall. She was wearing a green apron scattered with patches of flour and held a ladle in her left hand.

"This is Laura, Andrew's wife," my host made the next introduction to me. The woman wasn't as impassive in her greeting as her spouse, raising the semblance of a smile in her craggy, aged face, but was far from overwhelmed by my arrival.

"Laura is an amazing cook," Lawrence placed his arm around her shoulders, which made the woman look distinctly uncomfortable. I gained the impression husband and wife bore some sort of resentment towards us.

She ducked from under Lawrence's embrace and returned down the passageway.

"Where did you find them?" I whispered to him. They didn't look like people he would choose to suit his outgoing personality.

"They're old family retainers. I'll tell you about it later," he whispered back, then walked across to one of the doors off the hall.

"Come in here," he opened it. "This is the former sitting room."

More dark panelling surrounded the large room with a bay window at the far end. It was empty apart from a brown leather sofa and a couple of armchairs.

The broad fireplace was ornately fashioned with a carved wood mantelpiece surround. Above it hung the portrait of a middle-aged man with a bushy, dark moustache and neat side parted hair. He stared down at us austerely, an air of superiority in his gaze. Lawrence saw me studying the oil painting.

"That's the late Lord Ernest Loftbury. A gentleman of the English aristocracy and the last in a long bloodline to own the island."

An uneasy feeling that the lord in the portrait was somehow not gone from the place came over me. His image seemed so alive. Penetrating, calculating eyes.

"This will make a great conference room," Lawrence surveyed the setting, his enthusiasm unbounded.

"Conference room?" I was puzzled.

"Yes, I plan to turn the place into a getaway for businesses. Where executives can find relaxation as well as getting down to the nitty gritty of sales expansion strategies. An island retreat."

"It's not exactly a sunny isle," I pointed out.

"That's the point." Lawrence walked across to the bay window overlooking the side of the property. "It's for mental and physical toning. There's another large ground floor room that I'll convert into a gym and sauna. And another for a swimming pool. This place is enormous. Twenty upstairs bedrooms alone."

His imagination was soaring. I had to admire his get up and go.

"And, of course, loads of room on the island for a boot camp, outward bound, golfing, tennis and sailing from the bay. The potential's enormous." He paused. "But there's a lot to clear up and renovate first."

I joined him at the bay window. The large lawn outside and flower beds were overgrown with weeds.

"But it can all be done."

At that moment Laura entered the room with a tray of coffee and cakes, placing it on a small table in front of the sofa.

"Let's have a quick bite and drink, then I'll take you for a tour round the island in the launch before it gets dark."

As we settled down on the sofa for the snack, I felt distinctly uncomfortable with Lord Loftbury staring at us from the portrait.

****

Thankfully the seawater around the island had calmed since my arrival as Lawrence took me for the circular tour. The mist had lifted and the distant pine trees I'd seen from the bay were now clearly visible as we soared past the forest rising majestically on a hillside above.

The far end of the island stretched into a rocky peninsula, the sea breaking into sprays of white surf as it hit the rocks. Some of the hills further inland were covered in clusters of heather. Certainly it would be a great place for the outdoor activities Lawrence had in mind.

As we made the return journey along the other side of the isle, Lawrence allowed me to steer the motor launch, giving me a quick lesson on its manoeuvrability and instruments. It was the first time I'd 'captained' a launch of this size and after a few corrections took to it fairly quickly.

CHAPTER 2

THAT evening, Laura served us a fantastic roast beef dinner. Lawrence was right about her culinary skills. We ate in another large downstairs panelled room. Once again it was almost bare save for a ridiculously long, polished mahogany table with regency chairs lining each side. Lawrence and I sat opposite each other at one end.

The wealthy people who had lived here in the past, must have used it for lordly entertaining dressed up in their finery. There was also a portrait above the broad fireplace in this room. A woman with swept back auburn hair, soft brown eyes gleaming in a gentle smile, and a ruby red satin dress across her shoulders. Her gaze was entrancing.

Again Lawrence could see my interest in the oil painting.

"That's Lady Margaret Loftbury. Wife of the late Lord Loftbury," he informed me, raising a slice of roast beef on his fork. "Beautiful isn't she?" He paused. "Or was."

"Or was?" I was curious.

Lawrence lowered the fork.

"It's said that Lord and Lady Loftbury fell out. Over money. Or rather his lack of it. The story is that she emigrated back to her family in Canada with their children Henry and Felicity." Lawrence ate the slice of beef.

"Thing is, no-one was ever able to make contact with mother or children again. Rumour spread that Lord Loftbury had murdered them and that they were buried somewhere on the island. But the police didn't take the rumour seriously. A year later Loftbury committed suicide in his bedroom on the first floor here. Hanged himself."

The story sent a chill through me. I was staying in a place that seemed to have a grim history. Not exactly the relaxing retreat I'd been hoping for.

"Yes, it's a couple of years now since he did himself in," Lawrence continued. "He had no other heirs, so the island and this grand house went up for sale. The place had been in the family for generations, a good few hundred years at least."

I looked at Lady Loftbury's portrait again, wondering if she had decided to keep her new location secret from her husband and the world, or if her husband really had murdered her and their children. She now appeared enigmatic, as if harbouring a confidence.

Andrew, my host's general handyman and servant, now entered the room. He was carrying a trifle, which he placed on the table between us. He wore a tail coat, white-shirt with winged collar and bow-tie. It seemed extremely formal for the two of us wearing open-neck shirts, chinos and jeans. The man's earlier robotic, emotionless manner continued.

Laura followed carrying two bowls, now wearing a black dress with a white apron over it.

"Shall I serve this, or will you help yourselves?" she asked, in a less than friendly tone.

"We haven't finished our main course yet Laura. I'll call you back in a minute and you can serve the trifle then," Lawrence barked at her.

"No, I'll serve the trifle in a minute," I interrupted. I felt uncomfortable with this servant and master scenario. And the couple looked as though they should be enjoying retirement not waiting on us.

Lawrence gave me a hard stare, looking annoyed at me countermanding his authority. Andrew and Laura looked sharply at me too, as if I was an upstart who had no rank in this situation.

Lawrence broke the tension, his affable manner rapidly returning.

"It's all right, we'll see to it," he told his two servants. "You can go back to your cottage now and leave the clearing up 'til tomorrow morning."

The couple left without a word.

"Sorry if I seemed a bit cross," Lawrence apologised to me. "But these two only seem to respond to straight orders."

"How come they're working here?" I was still puzzled by Lawrence's choice of staff.

"They came with the island," he explained. "They were Lord Loftbury's last remaining servants. They found his body hanging from a rope attached to a hook in the ceiling beam of his bedroom. Both of them had worked for his family all their life, and for Loftbury's father before them, back in the days when the house still had loads of servants and family all over the place."

Now I understood why Andrew was dressed so formally for serving dinner. It was probably a requirement from the earlier days. Old habits die hard.

"When I arrived here," Lawrence continued, "they were barely subsisting. Had a vegetable patch and some chickens. Virtually broke. I took them on, giving them a wage, food and allowing them to continue living in their cottage a few hundred yards from here."

"That was good of you," I said. Lawrence smiled, accepting the compliment.

"Trouble is, I'll have to sort something out. They don't fit in with my plans." His eyes pondered the dilemma.

"You mean your grand scheme?" I took a sip of the vintage Dom Perignon champagne he'd provided to mark my arrival.

"This used to be a getaway retreat for generations of the Loftbury family going back to the 18th century," Lawrence continued telling me the history. "Days when they were wealthy and lived in a grand house in London."

He took a sip of champagne.

"This place was like their holiday pad. They'd come with an army of servants to relax and go bird shooting. I think there was even a golf course on the island at one time."

I nodded towards the trifle, wondering if Lawrence wanted me to spoon some into his bowl. He nodded back and continued in full flow.

""But when the last Lord Loftbury inherited it, he mortgaged the estate and used it as collateral against his mounting gambling and bad investment debts. He'd lost the London home as his main residence through bad debts and ended up living here on the island permanently. As you can see, the place has been totally neglected."

After eating we returned to the sitting room where Lord Loftbury's steely gaze from the portrait burned into my back, as if punishment for deliberately choosing an armchair to sit with my back to him.

I took out my phone to give Rosie a call.

"Don't bother," said Lawrence. "There are no phone signals, Wi-Fi or landline connections here."

I was surprised and disappointed. I'd told Rosie I would call her that evening.

"How will you run the place as a conference centre without any connections?" I asked.

"I'm going through all the official motions to have a communication mast erected on the island. Taking a while, but I'm hopeful of getting there soon," he explained.

It occurred to me the room I'd been given and freshened up in before dinner had electric lighting.

"You're lucky at least to have electricity then," I remarked.

"It runs off a diesel generator in a small compound at the back of the house. No services from the mainland here," he said. "Sometimes the generator cuts out, but there's a utility room near the kitchen where I keep a torch, matches and candles if there's a problem."

I looked around the room and towards the long, gold drapes that had now been drawn across the tall window. The thought of being in here with Lord Loftbury staring down at me by shadowy candlelight was chilling.

"Most of the old wiring in the place was totally knackered. I've had it renewed in the areas I'm using right now, but most of the other rooms are in darkness at night. Lots of work yet to be done," he explained.

I was glad the bedroom Lawrence had given me on the first floor had been part of the new wiring refurb. As with the other rooms I'd seen, it contained the dark wood panelling, but with a new double bed, modern wardrobe and bedside table with a lamp.

The one unsettling aspect was a white, marble cherub attached to the far wall that peered down towards the bed. With small wings rising from the shoulder blades and wavy hair, the cherub's genial smile looked extremely creepy. It seemed more fitting for a gravestone monument than a bedroom.

Maybe the last occupants thought it was a form of blessing reigning down on them from the Almighty. To me it was distinctly spooky and would probably be terrifyingly ghostly by candlelight. I hoped we wouldn't get a power cut.

For another hour I chatted with Lawrence in the sitting room, reminiscing about our days back at the business college we'd attended.

"It wasn't my thing," I admitted to Lawrence.

"We all have talents in different ways," he replied in his usual upbeat way. "As it happens, I might be able to put some work your way. Pays brilliantly and would involve some overseas travel."

"Really? Doing what?" I was intrigued.

He took another drink of champagne from the second bottle of Dom Perignon he'd opened for us.

"Can't say right now. Still working on some plans. But I'm hoping to put it together in the near future." His mysterious reply was as far as he would go for now.

We chatted for a while longer then made our way up the grand, if time worn, stairway to our bedrooms on the first floor.

"Tomorrow I'll take you for a tour of the island in the Land Rover," Lawrence promised, and we bid each other goodnight.

That creepy cherub was smiling at me as I undressed. My only brief respite from its watchful eyes was in the bathroom, which Lawrence had installed by partitioning off a section of the room.

I settled in bed and turned off the bedside light. In the darkness I sensed the figure continuing to stare at me. An item from the past that Lawrence hadn't modernised in the bedroom was the old window frame. It rattled from the breeze outside, somehow emphasising the remote isolation of the island.

As I lay in the darkness with my eyes closed, thinking about the day, I felt the growing sensation of a presence in the room. Something other than the cherub watching me. My instinct was to bury myself under the quilt cover. But I told myself to stop being stupid, childlike. I opened my eyes, half expecting to see some unearthly figure standing in the room. But there was only the empty dark, and the rattling window.

I turned on the bedside light to see my companion cherub still smiling unnervingly at me. Settling down again, this time I left the light on. I didn't have to look at the figure by resting my head sideways. Not since a child had I slept with a light on in the room. The darkness here was strange, unsettling.

Sleep finally had its way with me. Then something woke me with a start. I don't know quite what. I had the distinct feeling there had been a noise. Voices in the corridor outside. Footsteps. I sat up, listening. Silence. Even the window was no longer rattling. I must have been dreaming. Sleep crept back.

****

A surprise was waiting when I went down to the dining room next morning. Only one place was laid for breakfast.

Andrew entered carrying a plate of bacon and eggs accompanied by his usual expressionless face.

"Mr Keating was called away in the night by some business associates. He apologises and hopes to be back by tomorrow," he announced.

I was disappointed and felt let down. Lawrence could at least have called me in the night to say. But then he probably didn't want to disturb my rest. Maybe his leaving was what had briefly woken me in the night.

The bacon and egg with toast was delicious, but I was now at a loose end and stranded.

"I suppose Lawrence has taken the motor launch?" I asked as Andrew returned to clear the table.

"No sir. His associates came in their own boat for him."

That was a relief. I felt I had a lifeline if I wanted to leave the island. Staying another night entirely alone in this house with its less than happy sounding history was increasingly starting to unnerve me. Especially with that bloody weird cherub figure staring at me all night.

And yet I had a curiosity to know what the rest of the house looked like. With Lawrence I'd only been shown an area of the property that had been made reasonably habitable again. I was interested to see some of the other rooms.

As Andrew finished clearing the table he told me lunch would be served at one o'clock. That if I needed anything before then, he and his wife Laura would be at their cottage a few minutes walk away.

My eyes wandered to the portrait of Lady Loftbury above the fireplace, smiling softly at me. Eyes seemed to be observing me wherever I went in this place.

Since Lawrence wasn't here to take me on the island tour in his Land Rover, I decided to look around the rest of the house.

On the first floor I chose the long corridor on the other side of the balcony from my bedroom. Little daylight reached here and the new electric wiring was yet to be installed. The faded brass doorknob to the first room along the passageway was loose. I turned it and opened the heavy wood door.

Inside it was almost dark. I could make out white sheets draped over furniture. The tall window curtains were drawn closed. I walked across to open them for more light. As I pulled them back, clouds of dust rose into the air making me sneeze. The room had obviously been abandoned some time ago.

Against one of the walls stood a bed covered by a sheet. Above it was a framed painting of the grand mansion house with a horse drawn carriage and rider outside the front entrance.

Although covered in dust, the painting was still distinct enough to show what the property must have looked like in its heyday. Possibly a hundred years or more ago. Unblemished, majestic stonework, and tall windows shining elegantly with pride. The room held a strong atmosphere of the past. People long dead who had spent part of their lives here.

Another couple of rooms I looked into were similarly abandoned under dust sheets.

Returning to the main stairway I went up to the second floor. This didn't seem to be as abandoned as the corridor below. The first room I entered was dusty, but not mired in it. The room was large, but the furniture wasn't covered with sheets. A dresser, wardrobe, writing bureau and double bed minus the mattress that had not been abandoned as long ago as the furniture in the other rooms.

A door led into an adjoining bathroom. The fittings were old, but had obviously been installed as an update some years back. Was this the master bedroom for the late Lord Loftbury and his wife?

I opened the top dresser drawer. Inside was a pearl necklace and two pearl earrings. I was about to pick the necklace up when the vision of Lady Loftbury looking at me from the portrait in the dining room entered my mind. Somehow it seemed to be telling me the jewellery was personal, not for strangers to touch.

My hand drew back. The sense of intrusion grew as if the woman was now present in the room, her husband standing by her side ready to beat the intruder who dared to invade their privacy.

I turned around half expecting to see their ghosts watching me. The room remained empty, but the feeling of their presence lingered.

Although Lawrence had told me it was believed Lady Loftbury had left her husband to return to Canada with their children, the alternative story that she'd been murdered by him ranked more strongly in my mind.

I obeyed the urge to quickly leave the room. But as I turned my eyes fell on a sturdy metal hook embedded in a wooden ceiling beam. For a second I froze. Was that the hook Lord Loftbury had used to tie a rope and hang himself? I shivered as the imaginary vision of a man dangling with a noose around his neck flashed into my head.

For now, I decided to leave my exploration of the house. The prospect of spending another night alone in the property grew even more daunting.

Since Lawrence's business associates had collected him by boat, the motor launch was still moored in the bay below. The brief lesson he'd given me on how to operate it during his round island tour, gave me enough confidence to be able to steer the launch to the mainland. I was of a mind to stay at a hotel back in the harbour setting of Tullochrie overnight and return when Lawrence was due back tomorrow. In fact I could get lunch there.

I made my way down the track at the side of the house to Andrew and Laura's cottage, a few hundred yards away, to tell them not to bother with making lunch. At the front of the cottage a small paved area contained pots of flowers that were starting to fade with the onset of autumn. A wooden bench rested against the wall under a latticed window with white net curtains.

I rapped on the door knocker. A dog began barking. Andrew answered, restraining an Alsatian by its collar. The animal growled and barked at me, wanting it seemed to plant its long, canine teeth into my flesh.

"Quiet!" Andrew ordered the dog. "Be quiet Cannon." The dog growled a little longer then drew back.

"Cannon. That's an unusual name," I remarked.

"That's because he shoots at things like one," Andrew enlightened me. I could believe it.

I told him there was no need to prepare lunch and that I was planning a trip to the mainland. Might even possibly stay there overnight and return tomorrow.

"As you wish," he replied. "If you're back before five today and want dinner, let me know." He shut the door.

I went back to the house, grabbed my travel bag with some clothes, just in case I decided to stay in Tullochrie, and made my way to the launch. It took me a few minutes to work out how to start the engine, then I was on my way.

Leaving the bay, I wasn't quite sure where the harbour town was located across the water. There was a slight mist and the mainland coastline appeared without any distinct features. But as I grew nearer I began to see some other boats moving away and towards a certain point. This gave me a steer to the harbour. Thankfully the sea was calm, sparing me a bone-shaking crossing.

I berthed the vessel at the same point in the harbour where Lawrence had set off yesterday, scraping the boat only slightly on the jetty wall, but overall well pleased with my newly acquired nautical skills. Then I made my way to the harbour front pub where we'd met.

Another joy of arriving on the mainland was being able to pick up a phone signal. Now I could call Rosie.

Inside the pub I ordered a pint of beer and a beefburger, then sat down to ring her. It was great to hear her voice again.

"A guest speaker had to cancel, so my training course is finishing shortly," she told me.

"You're only sixty miles from Tullochrie. Why don't you drive over and spend the night with me on Lawrence's island," I suggested. The idea was spontaneous. I felt sure Lawrence wouldn't mind. And it would be wonderful having a close friend by my side without needing to spend the night alone in the house.

"Well the weekend's coming up, so why not," Rosie agreed.

"I'll be at the harbour front."

"Okay. I'll see you in a couple of hours. Got to go now." Rosie hung up.

After finishing the beer and beefburger I wandered round the harbour for a while. I imagined the cottages overlooking it were once occupied by fishermen's families in the days when the fishing industry formed the heart of the community.

But they were days long gone, Now there were bed and breakfast signs in many of the windows. Tourism was probably the mainstay of the area these days, with beautiful mountain and lakeland scenery as well as the sea nearby. Being October though, the main holiday season was over for now.

Down a side street I wandered into a couple of gift shops and then spent a while in a small museum featuring the history of the town when it was a seafaring community. As I left my phone rang. Rosie had pulled up in the car park behind the harbour. I went to find her.

She looked beautiful, her light brown hair tied back in a bun and a warm smiling face. She was still dressed in her formal dark jacket and skirt from the training course. We had coffee and toasted tea cakes in a café just along from the pub.

"Lawrence has bought the island?" Rosie was awestruck by the fact. She'd met him only once when we'd gone together to one of the lavish parties he sometimes threw. But she knew about him mostly from stories I'd told her of our days at the business college.

"He went on to be successful," I said, steeping myself in self-pity for a moment.

"But you have other talents," Rosie took my arm.

"Which ones?" I asked.

"I'll tell you when I find them," she laughed. It was infectious and I couldn't resist laughing too.

Rosie revelled at the boat crossing.

"I take it this is Lawrence's motor launch as well?" she called, the vessel cutting through the waves, the rushing air rippling her clothes while she stood beside me at the wheel.

"Certainly is," I shouted to make myself heard above the engine and thrashing seawater.

Mist was beginning to descend again and I was glad there was still enough visibility to safely steer the launch into the island bay. If it had grown any denser, I'd likely be wandering around lost in a foggy blindness. The craft had radar, but I'd had no lessons in using it.

When we arrived at the house I showed Rosie the dining and sitting rooms. She too thought the portrait of Lord Loftbury was a bit on the menacing side. As she looked at the painting of Lady Loftbury her face fell.

"There's a sadness in those eyes, but she looks so kindly."

I told her the story that went with the couple and the rumour that she and the children had been murdered by him.

"That sounds terrible. You don't think this place is haunted do you?" Rosie looked apprehensive.

"No." I attempted to allay her fear. But in truth, I wasn't absolutely sure myself.

We went up to my room. Rosie almost turned to leave when she saw that creepy cherub smiling at us.

"My God! That is spooky."

"It's just marble figure. Nothing to worry about," I played it down. She was right, but I didn't want her to go.

As she started unpacking her things, I said I'd walk to Andrew and Laura's cottage to ask if they would serve us dinner. It was before five o'clock.

"No. You're not going to leave me here on my own," she insisted. "Not with *that* staring all the time!" She pointed at the cherub. I waited until she'd unpacked and freshened up.

We walked to the cottage together and I warned Rosie that a snarling Alsatian might be eager to greet us.

I knocked on the door and barking started. Laura opened it. Fortunately this time the dog was safely confined somewhere inside the property, from where I could hear Andrew ordering the animal to be quiet.

Laura studied Rosie quizzically. I introduced her. The woman just nodded.

"Would you be so kind as to serve dinner for Rosie and me this evening?" I asked.

Laura nodded again.

"Seven o'clock." She closed the door.

"Sociable type," Rosie remarked wryly as we began walking back to the house.

"Perhaps isolation has an effect," I replied.

We had a bit of time before dinner so I suggested taking a look at some of the other rooms I hadn't seen in the house.

We made our way to the second floor and along the corridor with the room where Lord Loftbury may well have hanged himself. On this occasion though I steered clear of it. For one there was something uncanny about the atmosphere and two, if the cherub in my room gave Rosie the abdabs, the hanging hook in the bedroom would probably cause her to pack and leave.

Passing that room, we opened a door further down the passageway. The door handle was loose and squeaked as I turned it. Once again the curtains were drawn closed and another dust cloud rose as I pulled them back to let in light.

And again the furniture was also covered in dust sheets. One of them covered a single bed.

In a corner, Rosie pulled back a sheet to reveal a box containing some toys. A tank, a collection of soldiers and some racing cars. Another box contained a jigsaw puzzle, an illustrated science book and some certificates for writing and arithmetic achievements from a school in Edinburgh, Scotland.

We assumed this must have been the bedroom of the Loftbury's young son, Henry, and the certificates likely from a boarding school they must have sent him to in the mainland city of Edinburgh.

We left the room and started to approach another door opposite. Just as I was about to open it, we heard the voices of a boy and girl talking inside. It sounded as though they were arguing about something. Indistinct, but like 'no that's mine, leave it alone'. Then silence.

I hesitated to open the door. Rosie and I looked at each other. Puzzled. Wondering if it was just the one of us who'd heard the voices. Our glances confirmed we both had.

Slowly I opened the door. I really didn't want to, but was driven by immense curiosity. Maybe there *were* children inside. God knows why. But maybe.

The room was dark. The curtains drawn closed. Rosie stood behind me as I strained my eyes in near darkness to see if anyone was present. The silence was eerie. The setting empty save for more dust sheets over furniture including another single bed. I crossed to the curtains and opened them.

Rosie remained standing near the open door, reluctant to enter any further. Above the bed was a framed print. I walked across to it and wiped away the coating of dust covering the image. It showed a young girl with fair hair and a beaming smile on her face, standing in a field beside a pony. It didn't take much to guess that this was probably the bedroom of the Loftbury's daughter Felicity.

"Let's leave. This room is giving me weird vibes," Rosie called from the door. "Do we have to carry on with this? I'm not sure I want to stay."

"Let's just look a bit further. I think we're just spooking ourselves because the place looks run down." I was determined not to let my fears get the better of me.

Reluctantly Rosie followed me to the end of the passage where we saw a narrow, spiral wooden staircase leading up to what I presumed must be an attic room. Rosie waited while I made my way up the stairs, each one creaking underfoot until I reached a short platform leading to the door at the top. I turned the handle, but the door was locked.

"Probably the servants' quarters back in the old days," I remarked to Rosie as I descended the stairs.

"I want to leave this floor." She looked troubled. "There's something not right about the atmosphere. As if things are watching us."

I knew exactly how she felt.

"And what about those children's voices we heard," she whispered.

"Might have been the wind blowing outside. It can create strange sounds through small gaps in the windows of old properties like this," I offered an explanation.

Rosie didn't seem convinced, and I can't say I'd reassured myself either.

In the short time left before dinner we took a stroll in the large garden at the side of the house.

A paved pathway dividing lawns on each side led to a fountain with a unicorn as the centrepiece. It looked as if water once spouted from the unicorn's mouth into a circular pool below. But now the fountain was dry and the unicorn blemished with lichen, the pool sprouting weeds from a layer of dirt and mould.

The lawns, which once must have looked magnificent, were also overgrown with weeds spreading across to invade the raised flower beds bordering the edges.

Twilight was rapidly fading towards darkness so we went back inside to the dining room. It was a little before seven, but Andrew came through the connecting door from the kitchen ready to serve us. Once again he was in formal wear for the occasion and I noticed Rosie turning her head aside to suppress a giggle at this immense overdressing for the occasion. Andrew placed starters of smoked salmon with melon slices on the table for us.

"I feel very important," Rosie whispered as he left the room.

A little later Andrew brought in the main course of lamb cutlets with a selection of vegetables.

"Your wife is an amazing cook," I complimented. "Where do you get your supplies?"

Andrew replied in his same expressionless manner.

"We grow some vegetables ourselves and some of our supplies come from the mainland." At that he turned and left the room.

Rosie laughed again.

"I think this island's been taken over by robots."

I almost replied by saying more likely it's been taken over by ghosts, but stopped short not wanting to unsettle her again. After all nothing had happened to prove there were unnatural manifestations in the place. The children's voices were a weird thing. But I refused to believe they came from ghosts. There had to be some logical explanation although presently it escaped me.

After finishing a dessert of delicious apple crumble with custard, we returned to my room. That ogling cherub was still unsettling Rosie, so I took one of my shirts and covered it.

Rosie looked extremely desirable in the cream blouse and black skirt she was wearing and I took her in my arms for a long, exploring tongue kiss. Her breasts pressing against my chest added to the pounding desire to pleasure and enter her delicious vagina. I began kissing the nape of her neck. She sighed, urging me on. Then she pulled away.

"Come on! Get your clothes off, let's get into bed," she beckoned.

Swiftly undressing we climbed in together. I was about to caress her again when she abruptly sat up.

"Turn that bloody bedside light off. I can feel that weird cherub thing staring at us through your shirt."

I obeyed, plunging us into the privacy of darkness and starting to kiss her again, teasing her breast nipples with my tongue. Slipping my hand down to her opening, stroking, enjoying the sighs of pleasure coursing through her body. I raised myself to enter her softness.

She screamed, pushing me away violently.

"What's wrong?" I was mystified, fearing I'd hurt her in some way.

"There was a woman standing by the bed. Looking at us." Rosie's voice was quivering in terror. I quickly turned on the bedside light.

"A woman?" Now I was even more mystified.

"She was standing there," Rosie pointed to the spot beside us. She scrambled out of bed and sat on the side clutching her forehead in anguish.

"This place is fucking haunted," she said. "I don't want to stay here a minute longer."

"You sure you didn't just imagine it?" I asked, getting out of bed and looking round the room in case some intruder was hiding. But other than us, the room was empty.

"I didn't fucking image it!" Rosie sounded angry that I doubted her word. She stood up and started gathering her clothes from the floor to get dressed.

"What did she look like?" I asked.

"I didn't study her. I was terrified. "Her hair was sort of..." Rosie paused as some revelation seemed to strike her.

"Her hair was like in the style of the woman in the portrait downstairs. Sort of swept back." Rosie paused again.

"Christ, it's her ghost isn't it! That rumour about her being murdered with her children. It's true isn't it?" She was beginning to panic.

I held her in my arms.

"Steady," I whispered to calm her. She relaxed a little.

Rosie was not one normally influenced by flights of fantasy, though there was a very strange atmosphere about the house. For now I thought the story of murder had conjured up the spectre in her imagination. She'd seen the portrait of Lady Loftbury and that could have played tricks with her mind. But she was upset, and I had to reassure her without saying I doubted her word.

"I just want to get out of this bloody place," she finished dressing and began collecting her cosmetics and toiletries, placing them in the travel bag.

"I can't take you back to the mainland right now. It's still dark and we'd get hopelessly lost at sea," I explained.

"Well I don't want to stay in this room. It's bloody haunted." Rosie was deeply distressed. I got dressed and we went downstairs.

Waiting in the dining room for first light would confront her with the portrait of Lady Loftbury. That would not be a good idea in Rosie's present state. Nor the prospect of having the haughty painting of Lord Loftbury staring down at us in the sitting room.

I decided on the kitchen which I hadn't seen so far. I guessed there would be no paintings in there.

One access to it was through the dining room, but that was to be avoided. Laura had come to greet me from a passage off the reception hall, so we walked down there and found a door into the kitchen.

It was a large area with a mixture of old and new. A broad, cast iron range with a pile of logs beside it spanned most of the far wall. To the side was an arched brick fireplace with a metal bar stretching across the inside. This I presumed would have once suspended a cauldron with broth over an open fire. Now it no longer looked in use.

Fairly modern kitchen counters were installed with pine cupboards on the walls, though they all looked scuffed and tired and in need of replacing.

In the centre was a long wooden table for food preparation, pots and crockery stacked on it. The surrounding original brick walls had been covered in cream emulsion in an attempt to give the room a more modern look, though a lot of the paint was now flaking. The fridge and microwave didn't look quite right in the setting.

A couple of chairs were tucked under the long table and I pulled one out for Rosie to sit. I opened some of the cupboards and found a jar of coffee and a couple of cups, filled the kettle at the stone sink and joined Rosie at the table.

It was only ten thirty and it would be at least another seven hours before there would be enough light for me to see my way back to the mainland in the launch.

We chatted for a while as I recalled the times we'd spent together back home in London. Friends, theatre, concerts, museums and my old chestnut of trying to persuade her to live with me. But she wasn't ready for that. Still enjoyed her own independence. That subject started to stir her emotions. It was a sensitive area. The last thing I wanted right now was to stray into subjects that could lead to conflict and upset. Her nerves were jangled enough.

After a while Rosie stood up and walked round the kitchen trying to imagine what it must have been like in the old days when the place was teeming with servants.

There was a tea towel over the handle of the range. I placed it across my arm and pretended to be a butler.

Rosie laughed. That pleased me.

"Then make me another coffee servant," she ordered.

I was about to obey when we heard a shout. It echoed indistinctly, but like a woman's urgent cry for help. Anchored to the spot, we stared at each other totally thrown by the sound.

"Stay here," I said, raising my hand.

Cautiously opening the door to the passage, I glanced each way but could see no-one. I walked into the reception hall and took the opposite passage running beneath the stairway. There was only one light a few feet down. The remainder of the corridor faded into darkness.

"Hello. Anyone there?" I called.

Silence.

I climbed the stairway to the first floor and called out again. Still silence.

On the second floor there were no lights along the corridors. Lawrence hadn't had this floor rewired. I'd need a torch or candle from the storeroom near the kitchen. But in truth, my nerve was starting to fail me.

I was looking into the darkness of the corridor where in the daytime I'd entered what appeared to be Lord and Lady Loftbury's bedroom. That hook hanging from the ceiling beam, which I convinced myself he must have used to hang himself. The vision I'd imagined of him swinging there again floated into my mind.

Now I began to sense invisible eyes peering at me. Spirits of the past curious to know what intruder was disturbing the privacy of their home. I didn't know from where the shout had come, but it was becoming obvious there was no-one else in the house other than Rosie and me.

As I began to turn my gaze away from the pitch black of the corridor, I caught the glimpse of an illuminated figure at the far end. At least I thought it was. Just the merest fragment of movement. I stared hard, my heart beginning to pound. Was it an intruder? Or a ghost? Maybe Rosie really had seen the spirit of Lady Loftbury standing beside the bed. Now I felt goose bumps rising on my skin.

"Hello. Anyone there?" I called again. Still silence. Should I return downstairs and get a torch? It was hardly likely tramps would be making a special journey to the island to find a bed here. And even less so in the middle of the night. The likelihood of anyone else being here was remote. Other than ghosts. The thought chilled. Andrew and Laura would surely have responded to my calls if they'd been present.

I went back downstairs to Rosie.

"Did you see anyone?" She stood by the kitchen range looking worried.

I shook my head.

"I need to get out of this place." She came to me, taking my hands and pleading earnestly. "You need to as well. This house is evil. I can feel it."

It was a tempting thought. I could pack my things and leave the island with Rosie at daybreak.

"I can't just go without a word to Lawrence," I said.

"Well he left you here to go off somewhere."

Rosie was right.

"Yes, but he's a busy businessman. I expect something urgent came up." It felt disloyal to ditch an old friend's hospitality on the spur of the moment.

"I'll take you back to the mainland then return to see Lawrence. He's due back tomorrow. I'll say something's come up and I need to return home to London." My compromise seemed to satisfy Rosie.

I made us another coffee and we chatted about our families. Rosie's mother and father who were taking an autumn holiday in Venice, and my younger brother, Justin, who was at university working on a science degree. He was the shining academic of the family.

Our minds weren't entirely concentrating on the conversation though. I think both of us were half anticipating another shout or some inexplicable sound to break out in the house.

"Let's go outside," Rosie voiced her unease. "I just want to get out of here." She put on her black leather jacket and picked up her travel bag. I took the bag from her hand and carried it.

Outside the night air felt chilly, though refreshing away from the foreboding atmosphere in the mansion house.

The moon shone vividly in the clear sky, illuminating the bay below in a silvery glow, the waves breaking softly on the shingle shore. The motor launch was clearly lit, bobbing gently at its mooring beside the jetty.

I placed my arm around Rosie's shoulders. She rested her head on me. For a moment all seemed peaceful, in tune with the beauty of nature.

"Let's get on board the boat," I suggested after a few minutes. We walked down the sloping path to the jetty, gravel crunching loudly underfoot in the quiet of the night.

As we climbed aboard I looked back. The mansion house towered in the moonlight, like a monster peering down at its prey. The ungodly deformities of the gargoyles on the corners were highlighted in the glow, as if awaiting a command to leap from the high ledge and tear us to shreds for daring to leave.

With relief we climbed aboard the boat, offering sanctuary from the brooding building.

Inside the cabin red upholstered lounge seats ran its length on both sides with a light brown table between them. A little further along a short flight of steps led down to a small galley.

A relaxing tiredness overtook us as we each took a side on the seats. Our unsettling vigil in the house had driven out all feeling of rest. Away from the place it was catching up. There were several more hours to go until sunrise, so we spread ourselves across the seats and with the cradling sway of the boat soon fell asleep.

CHAPTER 3

WHEN I woke, light was streaming through the cabin portholes. Rosie was still sleeping. I looked at her for a moment. Her face so peaceful, her dishevelled hair enhancing her beauty.

But morning had come. Time to take her back to the mainland. I glanced at my watch. 7.45. I softly shook her. For a second she was puzzled, swiftly assessing her surroundings. I kissed her forehead then left to start the engine.

The sea was still calm as we made the mainland crossing. Rosie joined me at the wheel, bracing fresh wind in our faces lifting our spirits.

The café in the harbour was open so we went in for breakfast. Rosie a bowl of cereal and scrambled egg with toast. For me, egg and bacon.

As we headed to the car park, I began to feel sad. I'd really wanted Rosie to enjoy her stay on the island. But it was not to be. And now my companion and lover was leaving me. Of course, it was a self-imposed exile in loyalty to my friend Lawrence. But it wouldn't be for long. Or so I thought at the time.

"When Lawrence returns today, I'll tell him something's come up and I have to leave," I assured Rosie as she placed her travel bag in the boot of her car. "I'll drive back to London later and come over to see you tomorrow."

We kissed, a long lingering moment. Then Rosie climbed into the car blowing another kiss through the open window before driving away.

On my return to the island, the house didn't seem quite so menacing as in the moon glow the night before. Now it seemed to be patiently waiting, biding its time.

I was expecting Andrew to appear wondering why I'd been missing for breakfast. Set mealtimes seemed to be a stock routine for him and his wife Laura.

Inside the house a strange quiet pervaded. I went into the dining room, but placings for breakfast weren't set. Not that I was hungry after eating breakfast on the mainland.

I entered the kitchen. The empty coffee cups Rosie and I had drunk from were still on the food preparation table. That appeared odd. Surely if Andrew and Laura had been there to prepare breakfast they would have removed them? Nothing seemed to have been moved since we'd left in the early hours. Where were Andrew and Laura?

I went upstairs to my bedroom to freshen up. That cherub was smiling knowingly at me. The shirt I'd placed over it to mask its gaze was laying in a crumpled heap below. It must have slipped off. At least I hoped that was the explanation.

After a refreshing wash I went back downstairs, wondering why Andrew and Laura were missing. And at what point Lawrence would return today. I was keen just to make my excuses to him and leave.

I walked the short distance down to Andrew and Laura's cottage to find out why they hadn't turned up.

Knocking on the door I waited for answer. None came. Not even the barking of their Alsatian dog. I knocked several times more. Still no reply. There was a brass knob in the centre of the door for pulling it shut, but no handle to open it. I pushed at the door a little, but it was locked. I'd need a key to get in.

Maybe a friend or family had arrived in a boat while I'd been away, and taken them to the mainland for the day. Or to get new supplies.

On the way back to the house I looked across the bay towards the open sea hoping I might see a launch with Lawrence returning. But apart from a distant ship on the horizon, the view was empty.

A gusty wind was picking up, the waves growing agitated and breaking into white surf as they rolled. I hoped Lawrence would be back soon. The thought of the sea growing too turbulent for safe crossing and stranding me alone on the island was not a welcome prospect.

I returned to my room. After the disturbed night I decided to rest for a while waiting for Lawrence.

Imagine my horror! The shirt that had fallen to the floor was now back over the cherub. I was sure I'd left it on the floor. Hadn't I? There was no-one else on the island as far as I could make out. Except perhaps...ghosts?

I could feel the cherub smiling through the shirt. Mocking me. I left the room quickly and went back downstairs to get out of the house. I was prepared to wait in the open until Lawrence returned. All day if necessary. But soon it looked like I wouldn't have to wait for long.

A launch appeared in the distance rapidly cutting through the waves towards the bay. I made my way down to the jetty to greet him.

As the red hulled craft with a light blue cabin drew nearer, I could make out a man steering and another standing by his side. Neither of them appeared to be Lawrence so I presumed he was inside the cabin.

I stood by the mooring as the launch pulled in. One of the men threw a rope asking me to tie it to the capstan. There was no sign of my friend.

"Where's Lawrence?" I asked as the two men joined me on the jetty, looking smartly businesslike in dark suits.

"Why, we're looking at him, aren't we?" The man's eyes looked sharply inquisitive, searching me suspiciously. He had an athletic build and moved sleekly as if capable of springing like a leopard without warning. His combed back chestnut hair was slightly ruffled from the crossing.

"I'm not Lawrence. My name's Alex. Alex Preston. I'm a friend of Lawrence."

The man looked at his companion, a giant well over six feet tall and probably half as broad. His face looked like it had taken some heavy blows in its time, misshapen from a broken jaw and cheekbones. The man's eyes were not sharp like his colleagues, just staring aggressively at me it seemed for an order to mash me to pulp.

If these were Lawrence's business partners, what sort of business was he involved with? The men were more like heavies, maybe even gangland.

"Well Lawrence, let's go up to the house and have a chat," the sleeker looking of the two continued.

"I'm not Lawrence," I protested. "He's not here."

"Well, if you don't want to use real names, I'm happy with that," he replied. "You can call me Jack. He looked over to his large associate. "And you can call him Eddie."

The giant eyed me, still waiting for the command to attack as he agitatedly rolled his knuckles in the palms of his hands.

The one who called himself Jack nodded in the direction of the house. I felt there was no other choice but to obey if I wanted to remain in one piece.

As we entered the main entrance hall Jack gave a soft whistle as he studied the setting.

"Needs a bit of work, but you've got yourself a grand palace here," he said.

"It's not mine. I'm not Lawrence," I continued to protest.

"Yes, you've said."

Jack walked across to the dining room door and opened it.

"Wow! This is some place to eat." He took in the expanse of the room and the long dining table.

His associate Eddie gave me a hard shove in the back to follow Jack into the room.

"Who's that?" Jack pointed to the portrait of Lady Loftbury.

"She's the woman who was married to the previous owner of the island," I replied.

"Lucky man," Jack said admiringly.

He opened the door leading into the kitchen, again carefully surveying the scene.

"Bet they had an army of servants running around here," he observed.

"Have you got servants, Lawrence?"

"I am not...."

"Lawrence," Jack finished my sentence.

He hoisted himself on to the edge of the food preparation table.

"Right. The time has come to stop fucking about." The easy going half smile he'd been carrying dissolved into a cold, hard stare.

"What happened to the consignment?"

"What consignment?"

I was totally thrown by his question. That scheming half smile returned as he read the puzzle in my face.

"Do you hear that Eddie? What consignment?"

Eddie had ripped open a packet of biscuits on the counter near the sink, leaning back and munching his way through them.

"D'ye want me to....?" Eddie looked for the command from his boss.

Jack raised his hand as if saying 'down boy'.

"I'm trying to do this nicely," the half smile hung as he stared at me again. "Our friends in America are very upset. They transferred the money to you, but the consignment failed to show up. Why?"

I remained mystified. No idea what he was talking about.

"Look, you really have mistaken me for Lawrence. I'm Alex Preston, Lawrence's friend. He invited me to stay over. I've no idea about any money or a consignment."

Jack looked down, pondering the next step.

"If you're not Lawrence, where is he?"

At last it seemed the man was listening to reason.

"He left last night. Called away on some urgent business," I explained.

Jack laughed.

"I've never heard that one before." He sprang to his feet, reached inside his jacket and pulled out a gun pointing the weapon at me. I nearly shit myself.

"What happened to the fucking consignment?" His face reddened with anger. He pressed the gun against my forehead. I started shaking. Struggling to get out words.

"I'll count to five." Jack started counting.

"I...I'm not...Lawr...Lawrence. I wish I could...help... help you. I can't."

As the words stuttered from me, Jack reached five. I squeezed my eyes tightly shut, dreading it was the last moment. Nothing happened. I opened my eyes. Jack had lowered the gun.

"Well, I suppose if ten million dollars had been transferred to my account for providing nothing, I'd try to bluff it out," Jack reasoned, looking across to Eddie who had just finished the packet of biscuits.

"Grab that," Jack pointed to a meat cleaver hanging on a wall hook by the counter. Eddie obliged, a smile rising on his face.

What the hell were they planning? It didn't look good.

Jack grabbed my right arm and forced the palm down flat on the table. Eddie approached with the cleaver. Now I was near pissing myself, trying to break out of Jack's grip, but it clamped me like an iron cuff.

"Haven't you seen Lawrence's photo? I'm not Lawrence!" I pleaded.

"We're just hired hands. We don't need photos. People usually confess to us in the end." Jack nodded to Eddie, now raising the cleaver to sever my hand.

Sweat poured from me, my shaking was uncontrollable.

"Jesus no!" I cried.

A woman's scream echoed from outside. A bloodcurdling cry for help. We all froze.

"What the hell was that?" Jack looked towards the door, releasing my arm.

"Go and see Eddie."

Jack's dogsbody left, clutching the cleaver.

"Who's the woman?" Jack demanded.

"There's no-one else in the house," I replied, still shaking and starting to massage my arm to restore circulation.

"You just keep lying don't you. There is someone else in the place. We just heard a woman scream."

The thought of telling him the house could well be haunted didn't seem like a good idea. That would sound too far fetched to even consider believing. He might shoot me dead on the spot.

He paced the kitchen for a moment or two, his mind working on the next move while keeping a watchful eye on me with the gun in readiness to use.

The kitchen door opened. Eddie stood there, his face pale and drawn.

"What's up?" Jack demanded.

Eddie spoke slowly in a state of shock, now holding the cleaver limply by his side.

"I saw a woman with two children on the landing upstairs. I ran up there and they stood staring at me. Then they disappeared. Right into thin air." The bold, strong Eddie who only minutes before was about to chop off my hand was visibly shaking.

"This place is fucking haunted. I've just seen ghosts!"

"Don't be bloody stupid!" Jack wouldn't have it. "There's no such thing. Been on the pills again?"

Jack turned to me.

"You stay here. If you're really not Lawrence then I reckon he's hiding somewhere in the house. Something's going on up there. Come on Eddie. Pull yourself together."

Jack made for the door, then turned back pointing the gun at me.

"You stay here. If you try and escape – your dead. I will find you."

He shoved Eddie back out the door and they left to go upstairs.

I'd no doubt someone like Jack might hunt me down if I tried to escape. On the other hand I didn't really fancy my chances of survival if I remained. Wiping out unwanted people I assumed was the trade mark of these two.

What exactly Lawrence was into I couldn't imagine, but it was obviously not legit business. However, right now I had more pressing concerns. If I could just quickly get to the motor launch, maybe I'd be able to outpace these two heavies and make a swift escape to the mainland.

I quietly opened the door leading into the rear passageway and tiptoed along to the entrance hall. Continuing to tiptoe across the hall I reached the front door.

"Stop!" Jack's voice rang out. He was looking down from the second floor balcony pointing the gun at me.

Swiftly I pulled the door open as a shot echoed. The bullet struck the tiled floor just short of me, ricocheting upwards closely missing my head. I fled out the door.

Now I'd been seen, the problem was if I ran to the launch I'd be an open target down the slope to the jetty. I turned and bolted to the side of the building racing through the overgrown garden beneath my bedroom window. At the far end was a high hedge with an opening in the middle.

Sprinting with all my might I tore towards it. As I reached the opening another shot exploded narrowly missing me and ripping through the hedge leaves. Gaining brief cover from the hedge, another path beyond led past a derelict greenhouse with smashed windows. Further on a dilapidated shed veered into view. Then still further I entered an overgrown orchard.

I took cover behind a tree and looked back. Jack was directing Eddie to check round one side of the shed while he took the other. The pause gave me a bit more time. I ran across the orchard, in my panic continually catching my feet on the thick undergrowth.

Beyond lay a field rising into a small hill. No more cover. I raced across the field and ran as fast as I could up the slope hoping to descend on the other side out of sight before my attackers saw me.

Reaching the top, I glanced back. Jack and Eddie had just appeared from the orchard and caught sight of me. Another shot cracked through the air, but I was a good distance away and the bullet easily missed me as I moved on out of view.

At the top the ground was level for about a hundred yards. If they reached the summit before I could start descending I'd be a clear target. Racing furiously across the open terrain I reached the descent.

"Stop or I shoot!" Jack had reached the top not far behind me. I flung myself down the slope, escaping from his view as he fired another gunshot.

Stretching out before me at the bottom was yet another open field. Nowhere to take cover. Now all I could do was try to distance myself from any handgun accuracy. I was already breathless, but forced myself to keep running, stumbling often on the uneven turf.

As I briefly glanced back, the two men were running down the hill. Another crack echoed through the air. I'd put a good distance between us and was hopeful of being out of accurate target range, but they were determined to get me.

Ahead the field rose again into a small hill. I could veer off on the flat to the right, but it would afford me no cover at all. I began mounting the hill and was halfway up when another shot rang out, the bullet smacking into the slope only feet away. Another shot was dangerously closer as I reached the top of the hill and began running out of their sight down the other side. Now I was nearing exhaustion and wouldn't be able to keep going for much longer.

A few hundred yards away stood a large expanse of tall, dark green shrubs. A chance at last for cover. With the little strength I had left I tore towards it.

Reaching the spread of what I now recognised as rhododendrons, I glanced back again.

Jack and Eddie were descending the hill still heading my way. I plunged into the cloak of bushes, scrambling between the leafy branches desperately trying to hide myself in the tightly packed undergrowth.

Hoping I'd gone far enough inside I dropped down on the damp soil, praying my breathless panting wouldn't be heard. Soon I heard the rustling of leaves, trampling in the undergrowth. Jack and Eddie had arrived.

"We'll find you," Jack shouted. "You're a dead man if you don't come out now."

I was a dead man I reckoned if I did. I remained rigidly still, forcing myself to hardly breathe. The rustling continued as they searched for me. The sound began moving away. Maybe they wouldn't find me.

Then the rustling began approaching again, growing louder. This was it. They were going to find me helplessly sprawled on the ground. My heart was almost bursting through my chest. The rustling stopped.

"We will get you," Jack shouted. "You're on an island. Unless you're an amazing swimmer you won't get away. We'll be waiting."

The rustling of the leaves began fading again. They were leaving. But Jack was right. Swimming five miles to the mainland would be extremely dangerous. I could swim, but the waters in these parts were extremely cold. Hypothermia would likely kill me before I'd completed a mile or so, if the currents didn't pull me far out to sea first.

CHAPTER 4

I REMAINED still in the bushes for at least half-an-hour, worried that Jack and Eddie were trying to trick me into thinking they'd gone. Waiting outside for me to emerge.

When at last I moved, instead of back-tracking I carried on through the undergrowth until eventually coming out to see another stretch of open field. I'd be exposed again, so I waited a little longer to be certain my would be assassins were not present.

Cautiously I made my way across the open constantly looking round and praying they weren't still in pursuit.

It was starting to rain. Dark grey clouds rolled over the landscape. Already damp from laying in the rhododendron undergrowth, my shirt and trousers were becoming soaked.

I couldn't return to the house where my attackers would be waiting for me. And in the pursuit I'd lost track of my position on the island leaving me with no idea of the house's direction. In the space of a few hours I'd become a lost fugitive.

Now I had no idea what to do next other than try to find some sort of shelter from the increasing downpour.

In the distance a line of willow trees came into view. I headed for them. As I grew nearer I could see they were lining a small stream flowing at the bottom of a short, steep incline. But they offered little protection from the rain with the ground beneath their branches already becoming saturated

Since my clothes were now soaking wet I waded across the stream. At the top of the bank there was yet another open field, but now in the distance I could see a small, single-storey building. My hopes rose at the prospect of finding shelter and I headed in that direction.

Drawing closer, it turned out to be a weathered, yellow brick building about twenty feet long with a flat concrete roof covered in moss. I guessed the place must have been used for storing equipment in the earlier years when the island had a full quota of servants and estate workers. A wide rutted track ran past the structure.

The faded brown door was shut. I feared it might be locked as I tried the handle. It opened. Some luck at last.

The building was empty except for three large wooden crates lining the facing wall. I closed the door. A window beside it overlooked the field I'd just crossed. There were two bolts top and bottom of the door. I slid them shut feeling slightly more secure from attack by my would be killers. But it occurred to me the refuge could also turn into a trap. I'd have to keep alert to anyone approaching.

How long I'd have to stay here I had no idea, but at least my dripping wet clothes would have the chance to dry. The frenzy of the pursuit suddenly starting catching up with. I felt exhausted. Looking at my watch it was just after midday. I wondered what was inside the crates, but it would take something like a crowbar to open them, which was not exactly handy at that moment.

I leaned back on one of them for a moment to rest, but after a few minutes went to the window to make sure Jack and Eddie weren't heading this way. The day wore on with me desperately trying to relax, but continually wary of being caught out by my unwelcome visitors.

By four o'clock, feeling a little more certain they weren't coming this way, I hoisted myself on to one of the crates and laid down. The wood was marginally more comfortable to rest on than the cold, hard concrete floor. I needed to close my eyes, just for a short while.

Rattling on the door handle woke me abruptly. It was pitch dark. Someone was trying to get in. Terror gripped me. Jack and Eddie must have worked out I was here. Any second I expected to hear gunshot as they forced their way inside.

Silence fell. Were they playing a trick? Perhaps hoping I'd open the door to see who was there?

Quietly I slipped down from the crate. Maybe they'd assumed the place was empty. My eyes were growing accustomed to the darkness. A beam of moonlight suddenly illuminated a side wall through the window.

The door handle rattled again. It was clear someone was trying to get inside. Surely Jack and Eddie would have blasted away an entry.

Silence fell again as I tiptoed across to the window. I began to peep out when a face appeared staring at me. I recoiled in shock. Wild, wide eyes studied me. A spread of straggly hair. Mouth gaping in surprise. Then it was gone.

Quickly I looked out the window to see where the mystery figure was heading, but no-one was in sight. Who the hell was it? Apart from my pursuers I thought there was nobody else on the island. Perhaps Lawrence had returned. But the face I saw certainly wasn't his.

I looked at my watch in the beam of moonlight. It was nearly midnight. I'd slept for hours.

Waiting another ten minutes and certain as I could be all was quiet, I slid back the door bolts cautiously stepping outside. The thought of Jack and Eddie suddenly appearing by luring me into a false sense of security still made me jittery.

The rain had stopped and the full moon glowed brightly, reflecting in puddles along the rutted track running past the storehouse. I walked around the building. Behind it was a field and a few hundred yards beyond the silvery grey silhouette of a copse.

Whoever I'd seen at the window had completely disappeared. I stood for a moment enjoying the freshness of the clear night air. All was still and I could hear the faint sound of the sea brushing on an unseen shore of the island.

How could such a beautiful setting be casting the imminent threat of danger and death that seemed to be hanging over me?

Taking the side of caution, I returned to the storehouse and bolted the door. If I left now, even in moonlight I'd be wandering around entirely lost. My plan was to wait until sunrise before making the next move. I couldn't stay here forever. My mind kept wandering to the strange night visitor. Who on earth could it be?

****

I couldn't sleep again. Thoughts of the mystery man returning dogged me. Would he try to break in with violent motives? I needed to get off the island. My anticipated restful holiday had become a nightmare.

If only I could get to the launch, but that would involve being seen by my pursuers. I imagined they were at the house probably keeping a watchful eye by taking turns in shifts.

Swimming to the mainland being out of the question, the launch was my only realistic means of escape.

I guessed the track outside must lead to the house. Estate workers must have travelled from the bay to the storehouse with supplies or equipment from the mainland back in earlier times.

With no idea of how to retrace the earlier route of my escape from Jack and Eddie, I'd have to use the track to guide me back. At least that way I could hopefully sneak near the house and try to get to the launch unseen. That was the theory. I'd have to think on my feet as the actual moment drew near.

As the first faint glimmer of dawn appeared through the window I unbolted the door and carefully looked outside. Some rabbits were shuffling around in the field a short distance away. They stopped to look at me. Realising I wasn't approaching them they continued sniffing and nibbling the grass.

The track running past the storehouse looked more worn and rutted on the section to my right. This indicated greater use and was more likely to be the direction leading to the bay area. I had to chance my guess was correct.

The route curved as I travelled what I estimated to be a good half mile. All the while the streaky clouds grew lighter. Prying eyes would now be able to see me, and I was grateful beech and oak trees occasionally lined the track in case I needed to take cover behind them.

After what I judged to be another mile, the track curved sharply to my left at which point I could now see the back of the house in the distance. Soon I'd be in view of my enemy if they were looking out from an upper window.

I crossed a small wooden bridge over a stream and started progressing by darting where possible from tree to tree to avoid being seen. The sun was now lifting above the horizon.

Further along I could see the track ran past Andrew and Laura's cottage. I sprinted towards it praying I wouldn't be seen from a window in the house and took cover to the side of their property where the couple had a vegetable garden.

There was no sign of them, but if they were inside I thought it my duty to try and warn them that two killers were on the loose. That is, if they hadn't already found out to their cost. It was risky, but I went round to the front door and knocked. There was no reply. I tried once more. Still no reply. I couldn't drop a note through the door. I'd just have to leave it for now and try to get to the mainland where I could summon help.

The fear of Jack and Eddie suddenly appearing terrified me. I don't think they'd give me any second chance. Only torture and death.

Uncannily everything seemed too quiet, save for the cries of seagulls that frequently glided and swooped for fish below in the baywaters. My hope began to rise that perhaps my tormentors had left. But I couldn't take the chance. Now I'd have to sprint the few hundred yards to the jetty and pray I could swiftly start the launch and escape. The only catch would be if they were waiting for me in their own launch moored close by. The difficulty was that everywhere from now on was open for me to be seen and I'd have to rely on luck being with me.

I sprinted along the track then round to the right and down the slope towards the jetty. My heart soared. Then rapidly sank. Jack and Eddie's launch had gone. But so had Lawrence's. The jetty was empty. The gangsters must have towed it away or set it adrift. I was stranded here. Alone it seemed, except for that strange visitor I'd seen in the night.

My only hope now was that Lawrence had returned, dropped off by his business associates in their launch. If he was back, he wouldn't be happy his boat had gone. But then I wasn't happy with the mess he'd got me into.

Totally dejected, I made my way to the house. An unsettling air of gloom pervaded the entrance hall. The huge candelabra hung like a sword of Damocles above my head. Unseen eyes of spirits, condemned to wander restlessly in the confines, seemed to be watching my every move from the balconies above.

Rosie had claimed to see a woman beside my bed, and big Eddie had been reduced to a shaking wimp claiming to have seen the ghost of a woman. I wanted to leave this creepy place, but right now the house was my only refuge.

I shouted Lawrence's name several times, but was met only with silence as the echoes of my voice died down. It appeared he still hadn't returned.

It was nearly twenty four hours since I'd had a drink. I was desperately thirsty and made for the kitchen to have several glasses of refreshing water. At that moment the clear, cool liquid was sheer heaven, the greatest drink I'd ever downed. Although I hadn't eaten for some time either, I wasn't particularly hungry, but felt it necessary to eat just to keep going. In the fridge there was some cheese and sliced ham, which I ate straight from their wrappings.

My soaking clothes had dried on me, caked with dirt and dust. I longed for a shower. But more pressing was the mystery of why Lawrence hadn't yet returned. He'd been due back yesterday.

It was obvious from the visit by two heavies that he was into something illegal and with some unforgiving associates. But what? Had some other criminal gang got to him first and whisked him away on the first night I was here?

After refuelling with food I decided to go upstairs and take a look in his room. It was a couple of doors along the corridor from mine. Perhaps I could find some clues.

The door was unlocked. The room had been refurbished with cream walls, modern furniture and an en suite shower. Although there was ornate plasterwork coving around the ceiling, Lawrence enjoyed the fortune of not having a marble cherub gloating across the room.

His bed was unmade. Clothes were piled in a heap on a leather wing chair. An open laptop rested on a desk by the far wall.

Curiosity made me go across and turn it on. I sat down on the swivel chair as the screensaver lit up. For a moment I thought I'd need a password, but that obstacle didn't appear. Lawrence obviously felt secure with his island privacy. I clicked on the documents icon and a list of folders and files showed up.

I lost track of time as I opened them, growing more and more shocked and amazed at their content and the complex pattern of what was without doubt serious illegal activity in Lawrence's dealings.

Gradually I began to piece together his intricate web of Class A drug manufacturing and smuggling. Contacts in America. As I studied the documents and a series of emails I began to see a clearer picture of his dealings.

He was importing some powerful new deviant of cocaine from a small manufacturing unit based at a remote cottage in the Scottish Highlands. Supplies were transported from the mainland to the island for storage and onward transportation by sea.

There appeared to be an arrangement where a sea cruiser would call at the island at set dates and pick up consignments of the drug for smuggling into harbours on the Eastern seaboard of America.

Judging by some terse emails from the US recipients, the supply from Lawrence's end of the arrangement had stopped. But I couldn't see any return emails from him to explain why. Maybe the manufacturing unit in the Highlands had been raided. But if so, surely the police would have found their way here by now? Maybe it had just ceased operations. There was nothing to show the reason.

Now it fell into place. Why I'd had the unwelcome visit from Jack and Eddie, or whoever they really were. Lawrence must have received payment for some drugs, but for some reason failed to deliver. The two hit men certainly didn't have American accents. Jack's was Scottish, Glasgow area I guessed. Eddie's accent definitely came from London, south London likely.

They must have been sent by some UK connection to deliver revenge on behalf of the US interest. Lawrence couldn't have operated without relying on sophisticated criminal support for international drug smuggling. He was certainly a business guru, but not in the way I'd imagined.

Now a worse thought struck me. Did Lawrence know he'd be getting unwelcome visitors and invited me here as a stooge while he did a disappearing act? Then another thought came to me.

The last email Lawrence had received was dated the afternoon of my arrival on the island. If there was no signal connection here, how did it arrive?

I looked in the recess below the desk. A socket was attached to the skirting. Lawrence apparently had some signal link to a communications network. Maybe a satellite connection. Possibly a dish somewhere on the roof, or on the ledge at the back of the building.

Maybe I could connect with the mainland. Get a message to Rosie. I searched the room looking for the cable that could connect the laptop to the socket under the desk. But the search was fruitless. Either the connecting cable was well hidden, or Lawrence had taken it with him for some reason.

Normally I'd have thought it strange for a businessman to go off to a business meeting with his associates leaving his laptop behind. But in this case I imagined he wouldn't want the information on this one to fall into the wrong hands. Which also made me wonder why he'd left it open for the contents to be seen without any strict password access. He must have needed to leave in a great hurry, which added to my wondering if I'd been set up as his stooge while he made a hasty escape.

No surprise he was fabulously rich. I'd been admiring him for his business acumen. In fact he was a crook who made his wealth by exploiting drug addicts and no doubt helping to create new ones. My admiration for him had plummeted to the depths of disgust.

It puzzled me that Jack and Eddie hadn't searched the house and come across Lawrence's laptop. There was no sign of them turning the place over. Maybe Eddie had refused to return after seeing the spectre of the woman. Perhaps they'd decided to leave it for now and planned a return visit. My gut feeling was that they weren't giving up so easily. And unless I could get off the island my life was still imminently in danger.

I wondered what other secrets Lawrence hid in his room and opened the top drawer on the right side of the desk. It contained a notebook and a furniture brochure that appeared to be resting on something bulky. I lifted the brochure. Underneath it was a semi-automatic gun. I picked it up and examined it. The weapon had Walther P5 impressed on the side.

It took me a few minutes to work out the catches and safety lock and check that the weapon was loaded.

This was yet another big surprise courtesy of Lawrence, who was obviously prepared to encounter unwelcome visitors. The secret life of this man was revealing shocking revelations.

I was no expert at guns, my only previous experience at a shooting gallery several years earlier where I turned out to be a good shot. But shooting a target was nothing to prepare me for possibly shooting a living person. I wondered if I could do it if it came to the event. Now at least though, I had an added sense of security should my two mortal enemies decide to return.

I'd spent hours piecing together Lawrence's hidden life as a drug dealer. It was late afternoon and I felt weary. It was not everyday I'd been chased by killers and forced to hide in an old storehouse to later discover an old friend was a major criminal.

Taking the gun, I returned to my room. That cherub greeted me with the same smug smile, as if I was stupid and devoid of the higher wisdom. Only now its glossy marble eyes seemed to appear animated, the superior grin full of 'I know something that's going to happen'.

I took of my dusty shirt and covered its leering face, hoping this time the garment wouldn't mysteriously slip away to the floor again. I don't know if it was born of stress, but I was growing paranoid, actually beginning to believe that the cherub was possessed of a mischievous spirit.

CHAPTER 5

I UNDRESSED, glad to be rid of my fugitive clothing. After learning of Lawrence's secret life, my curiosity was now aroused as to what was inside the crates back at the storehouse.

But first I was going to freshen up under the generously wide shower in Lawrence's room, which was much more spacious than the smaller one in mine. He owed it to me at the very least.

As a friend he had put me in an impossible position. I felt I'd be betraying him by reporting his criminal activities to the police. On the other hand, in conscience I couldn't stand by knowing he traded in what I believed to be the death and destruction of innocent lives drawn into serious drug addiction.

And by remaining silent, I could find myself drawn into a long prison sentence just by association. I'd be guilty as an accomplice in a conspiracy if the police uncovered the network and discovered I hadn't told them all I knew. I wasn't looking forward to confronting Lawrence, if or when he returned.

Back in my room after taking the shower I was relieved to see the shirt was still in place over the cherub. Glancing out the window as I dressed, dark grey clouds were racing across the sky. Spots of rain dotted the glass pane and a strong wind was beginning to rattle the frame.

My plan to retrace the route along the track to the store-house and check what was inside the crates became less attractive. The rain was growing heavier. I'd just got over one unpleasant soaking, I didn't want another so soon.

Then I remembered being told by Lawrence that his Land Rover was in the garage at the back of the house. If I could find the keys, I'd be able to drive to the storehouse along the track.

After dressing I laid back on the bed for a while to get a short rest before setting off for the storehouse. It felt good to relax on a mattress after spending the night on a wooden crate and wondering if I might be hunted down and killed at any moment.

A tremendous crashing sound woke me. The wind howled at the window, rain whipping hard against the glass pane. The room was dark, then brilliantly illuminated for a second by a flash of lightning followed swiftly by a deafening boom of thunder. A storm raged overhead. I'd slept far longer than intended.

I switched on the bedside lamp. The shirt over the cherub had dropped to the floor and the creature smiled craftily at me. I leapt up just as a powerful gust of wind whacked into the window with such force I feared it would smash the glass in.

The bedside light flickered. The storm was probably affecting the diesel generator. Another lightning flash lit the window with a shuddering crack of thunder. The bedside light flickered and went out. I was plunged into darkness. Now the generator must have gone down.

One thing was still partially visible in the room. That bloody cherub, poised like a spectre in the shadowy glow of its white form, seeming to be one step away from coming to life as an evil spirit intending to drive me insane.

I seriously needed to find light. The only place I could think of was the store cupboard downstairs in the corridor opposite the kitchen. Lawrence had told me he kept candles and a torch in there.

The prospect of remaining in this house alone in the dark truly scared me. But I had to keep a grip.

My eyes were adjusting to the darkness and beyond that creepy cherub the vague outline of other objects was gradually coming into sight.

Opening the door, my hope that only the bedside lamp was at fault evaporated. The corridor light didn't come on either after feeling my way along the wall and flicking the switch.

Continuing to use the wall as my guide, I reached the opening to the stairway, carefully gripping the bannister to use it as a guide down the steps. At that moment another loud crash of thunder startled me.

My nerves were starting to sense presence all around. Those invisible eyes of past deceased residents curious to know what the intruder in their home was planning to do next. I fought against the growing urge to just plunge blindly down the stairway and get the hell out of the place as fast as possible, storm or not. But I didn't want to join their ranks by tripping and breaking my neck on the way down.

Gradually I reached the bottom. A flash of lightning through the two front windows in the reception hall gave me brief sight for the direction I needed. Carefully crossing the hall in darkness, I felt my way along the corridor at the back to the store cupboard. It was dimly lit by an emergency light in the ceiling.

A shelf to the left was stacked with candles. On a unit below lay a torch and beside it a box of matches. I put a couple of candles in my pocket and lit another. That would give me wider vision and the torch would be useful for longer distance viewing if needed.

The power of light restored my confidence. Now I could return to my room and wait for the raging storm to pass. Then at dawn I'd set off for the storeroom to see what was inside those crates.

I began making my way back across the hall when I heard children's laughter coming from one of the upper floors. I stopped to listen. The candlelight flickered, casting long shimmering shadows of the stair bannister across the side wall. For a moment all I could hear was the howling gale outside, rain flinging itself on the hall front windows and rumbling thunder in the background.

I must have imagined the laughter. The eeriness of this place was getting to me. I started towards the first step on the stairway when excited, young laughter from above broke out again, this time accompanied by the sound of running feet, as if children were playing a game of chase on one of the balconies.

Trying to suppress my fear of it being ghosts, I tried to reason that perhaps children really were in the house. Possibly relatives of Andrew and Laura who might have returned while I was in my room earlier and that the kids had secretly sneaked in here. But surely children of the living would have been frightened by the dark?

And there was nothing to suggest anyone else was on the island other than me and that strange man who'd peered in at the storehouse. He'd hardly be likely to sound like children playing.

Then came the sound of shouting from the upper floor.

"You'll ruin us all with your gambling!" a woman shrieked in anger.

"Be quiet, or I'll silence you woman!" a man's voice raged back.

The house fell silent again save for the furious storm rumbling and thundering outside.

My instinct continued urging me to flee, but curiosity to find out what was going on led me to stay. I began ascending the stairway, guided by the light of the candle. I clung to the belief there was a simple, logical explanation to what I'd heard.

Shadows leapt around me as the candle flame twisted and bowed in the air current.

I reached the first floor and was tempted to return to my room and lock myself in until morning. Then I heard a door slam shut on the floor above.

Standing still and listening for more activity, it entered my head that Lawrence might have secretly returned and for some reason best known to himself was playing a trick on me. From what I'd learned earlier, duplicity was not beyond him.

I called his name, but was met with silence. I decided to investigate and crossing the balcony climbed the steps to the second floor, shining the torch down the corridors on each side of the landing.

My heart began to race. Down the left side corridor the beam picked out a group of figures at the far end. For a second or two they were there, then gone. Now I seriously had doubts about continuing. If this was a Lawrence trick, it was bloody effective. I was determined to hold to reason and logic, but the resolve was rapidly slipping away.

This was the same corridor leading to what I believed to be Lord and Lady Loftbury's bedroom. The one with the hook in the ceiling beam from which I presumed he'd hanged himself.

I held the candle in my left hand and the torch in my right, carefully making my way along the corridor. The beam now picked out the bottom of the spiral stairway at the far end where I'd stood with Rosie just a couple of nights ago. How I wished she was beside me now.

Nearing the Loftbury's bedroom door, I began to sense a dreadful presence behind it just waiting for me to enter. I faltered for a moment, feeling that I could be approaching the point of no return.

Now only powerful curiosity made me carry on. But continue I did.

Nervously passing the door, a terrible feeling descended that I'd crossed the line into a horrifying trap. The way back had been closed and deep evil awaited.

It didn't take long for my fear to be realised. Just a short distance further along I heard the squeak of a door handle turning behind me. I spun round, the candle flame extinguishing from my sudden movement.

A man stepped into the corridor from that dreaded room. I shone the torch at him. It was the man in the portrait downstairs. Lord Loftbury!

He began striding purposefully down the corridor towards me, gripping a long handled axe in his right hand. He stared grimly through cold, hard eyes, sizing me as a target for the blade at his side.

I turned and started running down the corridor to escape and reached the spiral staircase. Loftbury was still approaching. I mounted the twisting steps and reached the short, narrow landing at the top.

Below I could see he was beginning to ascend the steps. Ahead of me stood a door. I turned the handle to escape inside, but it was locked. There was nowhere else to run. I was trapped.

His footsteps on the stairway echoed closer. He reached the top and stepped on to the landing, stopping only feet away and glaring menacingly at me. I shook in horror.

Gripping the handle with both hands, he raised the axe above his shoulders and began to advance again.

As he grew close I dropped the torch and raised my arms in self-defence, ready to try and take evasive action. The axe remained hoisted. Loftbury continued walking straight through me, totally unaware of my presence.

The door behind flew open. I turned. The room was lit. A woman and two children were cowering in terror against the facing wall, the boy and girl grasped protectively in the woman's arms.

"For God's sake don't!" the woman screamed.

Instinctively I sprang to try and save them, but the door slammed shut on me. I frantically pulled on the handle pushing hard, but it was locked again. I beat on the door desperately trying to stop the carnage I dreaded was about to happen.

A piercing scream rang out from inside the room. My blood curdled. I grew icy cold, every nerve in my body seemed shatter at the woman's horrific cry.

The pitiful sound echoed and faded away into total silence. I stood unable to move.

It took me several moments to regain my senses. I tried the door again. It opened. The beam of the torch I'd dropped was still shining and I picked it up. Now I was terrified of the scene I would see inside. Cautiously I pushed the door open wide.

The room was no longer lit. I shone the torch around. The setting appeared empty, just bare wooden floorboards and flaking paint on the walls. The woman and children I'd seen were gone. It came to me now that she was woman I'd seen in the dining room portrait downstairs. Lady Loftbury. In the drama my mind hadn't had time to make the connection. The children must have been the couple's son and daughter.

I searched the room to be sure no-one had just been in here, and much as I was trying to convince myself it wasn't true, there was no other explanation for what I'd seen other than ghosts. I'd seen ghosts. I believe I'd witnessed the re-enactment of Lord Loftbury about to murder his wife and children with an axe. The thought stunned me.

As the bizarre events were penetrating my mind, the torch beam lit a darkened area on the floorboards in front of the wall where I'd seen the woman and children quaking in fear. I couldn't be sure, but the dark brown stains in the wood reminded me of dried blood.

Now the horror of the event suddenly struck home. I felt sick and began to wretch. Suddenly I became aware of a presence in the room. Lord Loftbury stood a short distance away, smiling evilly at me. He raised the axe and began to approach, this time I sensed his target was definitely me. With a powerful swing the blade descended.

CHAPTER 6

DAYLIGHT shone through a small window in the room. I lay flat on my back, my limbs aching with stiffness. Where was I? I sat up and memory of what happened came flooding back. That axe descending on me.

I'd obviously passed out. Perhaps the ghost of Lord Loftbury was physically unable to harm me. I had no idea. Whatever the reason I was still alive.

Then the memory returned of witnessing the final harrowing moments of Lady Loftbury with her children. A mental scar that would haunt me for the rest of my life. I wanted to get out of the room as fast as possible. My watch showed half eight.

Collecting the torch, I passed the Loftbury bedroom fearing the evil spirit might suddenly reappear. Thankfully his ungodly presence appeared to be at rest for the moment.

Back in my room the expression on the cherub's face now seemed to be mocking me, almost saying 'you won't survive the horror of this house'.

I needed a drink. Preferably a strong one, but right now the imperative was to keep a clear head.

Putting on my black leather jacket I slipped Lawrence's gun into the right side pocket. As I made my way down to the kitchen, the landing and stairway seemed an entirely different place in daylight from the terror of the night. The storm had blown itself out and sunlight streamed through the windows each side of the front door. But still those invisible eyes all around pervaded.

The power to the fridge in the kitchen was off, though the orange drink I took from it tasted okay. I didn't feel hungry, but ate some cereal bars from a packet inside one of the cupboards just to keep going.

I presumed Lawrence's Land Rover was still in the garage at the back of the house. Probably there was an entrance to it from inside the building, but I didn't know where. So I set off to reach it from the outside. Maybe I could also find something in the garage to prise open the crates in the storehouse.

As I began walking round the side of the house I saw smashed pieces of concrete on the ground. Drawing closer I realised it was a shattered gargoyle toppled from the roof ledge. Part of its sinister face was still intact, snarling at me like an evil omen. It must have been struck by lightning in the storm, the loud blast that had awoken me in the night. Looking at the face sent a shiver down my spine.

Hurrying past, I reached the garage at the back, a large outbuilding attached to the property. Now I prayed the up and over door wasn't locked. My luck was in. I swung it open. The next potential obstacle was finding the key to start the Land Rover. It was in the ignition. Could this run of luck last?

Looking around for an implement to prise the crates open, I saw a workbench with spanners, a socket set and screwdrivers spread over it. But nothing heavy duty for prising. Then my eyes caught sight of a spade resting against the wall alongside. That would do. I placed it in the back of the Land Rover, started the engine and drove away.

The track alongside Andrew and Laura's cottage would lead me to the storehouse much quicker than my previous cross-country journey there, pursued by merciless killers.

Small branches were scattered along the route, victim to the ferocious storm that had raged in the night. As I approached the small bridge my hope of speedy progress suddenly confronted a new obstacle. A tree was laying across the track just in front of the bridge.

The stream had swollen to the size of a small river, the fast flowing current rising almost to the top of the steep embankment on either side. I'd have to cross the bridge on foot and walk the rest of the way.

I got out of the vehicle and then noticed a gap between the uprooted tree trunk and the bridge. Just wide enough to drive the vehicle through and over the bridge. Lucky moment number three. Perhaps all my wishes had now been granted, though I had a feeling more would be needed.

A short time later I pulled up outside the storehouse. Taking the spade from the back of the Land Rover I entered the building.

It took me a few minutes to lever open one of the wooden crates. I lifted the lid back and was surprised to see what lay inside. Bedding quilts wrapped in protective plastic wrapping. Why on earth would anyone, including Lawrence, want to store bed-ware in this storehouse? Maybe part of his plan for accommodation when the house was converted into a residential conference centre.

Of course, as the thought came into may head, I realised such a notion was nonsense. I lifted the quilts, searching deeper below. In the middle I saw something very different in plastic bags. White powder. I was no expert in drugs, and opening one of them to taste some of the powder like they do in films would make me no wiser.

It wasn't a huge leap of imagination to surmise it was some sort of class 'A' drug like heroin or cocaine, given the secret exploits of Lawrence that I'd discovered on his laptop. Also the fact it was hidden under bed linen. I guessed the other two crates hid the same, all stored for on-ward shipment. Jack and Eddie would have been thrilled to find these. And to think they'd come so close.

My bond of friendship with Lawrence would have to be broken. I couldn't know about this discovery and not in-form the authorities. Some small scale smuggling maybe I could overlook. Though I'd have to break all connection with him on that alone. But major drug running. That was a different league

I was glad I'd taken Lawrence's gun. With such high stakes, I began to think he would be prepared to kill me on his return in order to remain free.

I turned to leave. Standing at the open door was a man. The same straggly haired, wild eyed visitor I'd seen peering through the storehouse window the other night. For a second we stared at each other in surprise. Then the figure sped away. I leapt to the door to see him racing down the track in the opposite direction from the way I'd come.

That direction was unknown territory to me, but I had to find out who he was and why he was here. I started chasing after him.

He was fast and I struggled to keep up. After a short while he diverted off the path and started mounting a steep slope in the field. I followed him down the other side as he gained on me all the time. Ahead stood a forest of Scots pine trees that looked like the ones I'd seen in the misty distance when I first arrived on the island.

The man disappeared inside. I reached the trees fearing I'd lost him. Then I caught sight of the figure darting between the tall trunks. The evergreen foliage above made the surroundings darker as I entered the forest. It was difficult following him with scattered broken branches from the storm tripping me every so often. This man had amazing stamina as I felt my own energy beginning to flag a little.

At last he emerged from the trees into the open then seemed to disappear. As I reached the same spot at the edge of the forest, I saw a path descending down a rocky slope towards a bay below, surf breaking on the pebbly shore.

The mystery man was no longer in view and disappointment struck hard as my efforts now looked to be in vain.

Then I caught sight of him emerging from a rock outcrop below, still running like fury. I raced down the path which led to the beach. He'd disappeared again. I looked all around, standing just feet away from the tide rolling in.

Craggy rocks rose in a broad semi-circle surrounding the bay. I walked across the beach to a path rising upwards on the far side. It seemed to be the only other accessible route out of the bay.

My quarry must have been hiding. Suddenly he emerged again from behind a tall rock about a hundred feet further up the path. I was near spent, but determined to catch up with him.

The top of the incline was about another hundred feet further up from where I'd seen him. I reached the summit where the landscape opened on to yet another field. The man was nowhere in view. As if vanished into thin air. I slumped down on the grass, sweating and gasping for breath.

After five minutes or so and coming to terms with my disappointment, I got up and wandered into the field hoping I might catch sight of him again, but he was gone. It even crossed my mind that perhaps he was yet another island ghost. But I wasn't convinced a ghost would need to flee like that to escape from me. No this was a real person, though why he would be wandering the island I couldn't guess. It didn't make sense.

I turned to retrace my steps. It would be a gruelling slog back to the Land Rover. Then my eyes caught sight of movement across the field to my left. An animal. A dog. It was about a couple of hundred feet away. I could see it was vigorously tugging with its teeth at something on the ground.

Whose dog was it? The only dog I knew of on the island was Cannon, the Alsatian belonging to Andrew and Laura. I'd assumed they'd taken their pet with them when they'd gone to wherever they'd gone.

I walked towards the animal and saw a crude, makeshift barbed-wire fence stretched between posts cordoning off part of the area. A sign had been hammered into the ground reading: *Rock Fall – Keep Out*. The land appeared to be close to a cliff edge about fifty feet away.

I drew nearer, wondering what the dog was tugging. The animal caught sight of me. It stopped pulling at the thing for a moment and began barking furiously, warning me away as if it thought I was about to try and compete for the spoil. Whatever the object was, it looked like something long. Then the dog began tugging again.

As I continued to approach only the barbed-wire fence separated us, the animal less than twenty feet away. It began growling, every so often raising its head to eye me suspiciously as it carried on tugging. I might have left the creature alone, but now I could clearly see it *was* Cannon. I remembered a distinct white stripe that ran across the dog's head when I saw it at Andrew and Laura's cottage.

But more compelling at that moment was realising what the animal was trying to pull out of the ground. It looked a bit like an arm. I needed to see better.

The fence was a shoddy piece of workmanship and it was easy enough just to crawl under it. I drew closer to Cannon, who had now settled to tearing pieces off whatever it had found and chewing them. Its growling grew more threatening as I approached. Then the horror struck me. The dog was eating human flesh. It had unearthed a discoloured arm!

I came closer. Now the animal was truly aggravated. It dropped the grisly find and began seriously baying and growling at me, baring its ferociously sharp teeth and pre-paring to sprint for attack.

I called the dog by name, trying to calm it with soft spoken words of reassurance. For a second I thought it might work. At the sound of its name the animal stopped growling for a moment. But then I was a stranger. The animal wasn't convinced. It began baring its teeth wider, growing angrier.

If I hadn't seen what I thought was a human arm, I'd have definitely left there and then. But I had to check it out. This was serious stuff. And I couldn't just get on the phone to the police. I tried more calming words, but the dog wouldn't have it. The creature must have been starving.

Reaching inside my jacket pocket, I took out the gun. I had no intention of shooting the animal. It was a weapon of last resort and made me feel more secure. The dog seemed to pause for a moment, a curious look at what I'd introduced to the scene. But of course, it couldn't know what power of defence I held and resumed its aggressive stance.

Suddenly the animal raced furiously at me, vicious teeth bared, about to rip me to shreds. It leapt. In reflex I fired the gun. A loud crack. The dog whimpered in mid-air and hit my shoulder nearly knocking me over as it flew off sideways and hit the ground, rolling over and slumping lifeless a few feet away.

I felt absolutely terrible. My reflexes had just kicked in without any conscious thought. I went over and knelt down beside the animal, a trickle of blood seeping into its fur on the underside.

"I'm so sorry. Why didn't you just back off," I said, stroking the animal's still body, angry with myself and with this evil island, which seemed to be forcing me ever more towards insane thoughts and extremes.

After a few moments, knowing there was nothing I could do to restore the poor creature's life, I stood up and went over to investigate Cannon's find.

Yet more horror waited. It *was* a human arm. Half eaten. I paused, catching my breath, dreading what else I'd discover.

The ground had been freshly dug. I clawed at the soil and not far below the surface the top half of a body became visible. Just brushing away the earth from it sickened me. The body lay face upward, soil nested in the eyes, mouth and nose. As I continued to brush it away with my fingers, the full face began to emerge. Discoloured and beginning to decay with maggots writhing and crawling in its neck. Suddenly I recognised the facial features. *It was Lawrence!*

No wonder he hadn't returned. He'd never left the island. Not in life. It took me a few minutes for the realisation of this horrific find to sink in. All the time I thought he'd be back, he was laying here dead.

Who'd done this? Who had buried him? Had Jack and Eddie returned after hunting me to find Lawrence back on the island? Had they killed him? It's possible.

But how would they would have got here without transport? That puzzled me. I'm sure they never used the Land Rover to carry his dead body to this spot, or drive him here alive for execution. They'd have likely dumped the vehicle back outside the house and left without bothering to put it back in the garage if that was the case.

And it's highly unlikely they'd have walked here for the purpose. There must be some other explanation.

Right now all I knew was my need to desperately get away from this cursed island. As fast as possible. But I was trapped. No way out. No signals to contact the authorities, or Rosie. How I missed Rosie.

Perhaps she might be wondering why I hadn't returned home and contact someone to see if I was okay. But then I didn't always stick to plan. She probably thought I'd changed my mind and would return when I felt like it.

I scooped the soil back over Lawrence's body. In the grisly circumstances it seemed the respectful thing to do rather than just leave him exposed. His arm right arm was already badly chewed by Cannon. I covered that too. Not that any of it made any difference to him now.

I couldn't bury the dog. Instead, and totally inadequate though it seemed at that moment, I whispered a short prayer for both of the deceased.

CHAPTER 7

THE JOURNEY back to the Land Rover wasn't easy. As I descended the path returning to the beach, I saw the tide had come in further. The narrow stretch of pebbles I'd crossed earlier was under water. I clambered over the rocks behind, slipping frequently on the mounds of seaweed covering them. If I'd left it any longer this crossing would have been covered by the tide too.

By the time I reached the top of the path on the other side I was totally exhausted. And ahead was the pine forest stretching into the distance on either side. I had no idea what route I'd taken while pursuing the mystery man and stood there gazing at the trees feeling totally lost.

After a while I worked out where I'd emerged on to the field. I'd vaguely been aware that the sunlight had been breaking through the canopy of the trees high to my right.

The sun was still shining, but less distinct now, masked by a thin layer of milky cloud. It wouldn't have moved far in the time so I entered the forest now keeping its light to my left. Not the greatest navigation plan in the world, but the best available right now.

I wandered between the trees for an hour, hopelessly lost and beginning to think I would never emerge. A short time later I glimpsed an open field through the trunks ahead. I'd reached the edge somewhere.

Stepping out of the forest the field looked alien. I hadn't been here before. A couple of hundred yards ahead the land rose to yet another hill. This island seemed to be full of them.

Summoning my ebbing energy reserves I stumbled rather than walked to the top, hoping it would give me a good vantage point. It was a wise choice. In the distance I could see the storehouse and a miniature dot of the Land Rover beside it. But I'd have to trek what looked like another mile or two to get there.

By the time I arrived I was completely shattered. Climbing into the seat of the vehicle and resting there for some minutes, thoughts of the harrowing scene I'd not long left behind haunted me.

I started the engine and drove back along the track to the house, resolving never to go inside the property again. But tiredness, hunger and thirst were taking me over. Reluctantly I entered the front door and found some scraps of food in the kitchen and the last remaining carton of fruit juice.

Once again the nightmare encounters on this weird island left me coated in dirt and dust. I decided to take a shower in my room. But that would be the extent of my stay in the house. That night I'd sleep in the Land Rover and only go inside the property if the need arose.

Returning to the room, that leering cherub looked more cheerful than ever. The more I suffered, the happier it seemed. If I covered it, the covering would slip off the minute my back was turned. I'd had enough. My nerves were completely frayed.

I picked up the chair by the dresser and smashed it down on the cherub's smug little head. The chair shattered. The cherub remained untouched, smiling sanctimoniously, smugger than ever. God, how I needed to get out of this place. Why was I being punished like this? Either I was becoming paranoid or evil really was targeting me.

While I showered, the puzzle that had been festering in the back of my mind rose to the surface. Why had Andrew and Laura's dog Cannon been wandering on its own? Abandoned. Apparently so hungry it was prepared to root out Lawrence's body for food? If the couple had left the island, wouldn't they have taken their dog with them? Or arranged with me to have it looked after while they were gone?

I just had to rest for a while, and then I'd call at the cottage. Have a look around to see if the couple had returned or not. I set the phone alarm to wake me in case I fell into a deep sleep, then laid down on the bed. I wanted to avoid the terrifying prospect of waking here in the dark again. It was enough trying to rest in the presence of that bloody cherub gloating over me, let alone visitations by more ghosts.

****

I didn't need the alarm. With the events I'd witnessed, rest evaded me. My mind couldn't stop re-living the horrors. Half-an-hour later I got up from the bed. It was just after five in the evening.

Putting on my jacket, I set off on the short walk to Andrew and Laura's cottage. There was no sign of anyone being around. But I knocked on the front door in case the couple might have returned while I'd been away.

After knocking several times and getting no reply I decided that whether they were in or out I needed to look inside the cottage. The couple's non-appearance for several days seemed odd.

The door was still locked and I had no key to the place. My only option was to force the door, and if that didn't work use the gun to blast away the lock fitting.

Bracing myself, I rammed it hard with my shoulder. The door flew open and I nearly toppled over inside. It wasn't locked, just jammed against the frame.

A foul stench struck my nose as the cottage air rushed out. My eyes widened in horror at the scene that met me.

A seated body lay slumped with head and shoulders resting on the table. I stood transfixed for a moment, absorbing the shocking sight. Slowly, I started edging further into the room and saw another body laying on the floor at the other side of the table, as if it had tilted lifeless off the chair alongside.

This couldn't be happening. It must be a nightmare. But there was no relief of waking from a terrible dream. This was real.

Flies crawled and buzzed over the bodies which had begun to liquefy. But they weren't decomposed so much that I couldn't recognise them as Andrew and Laura. Dark brown congealed blood was spread down the sides of their heads.

My immediate thought was that Jack and his henchman Eddie had killed them. Then I noticed a revolver on the floor beside Andrew. What the hell had happened here?

On the table lay a white envelope, streaked with traces of dry bloodstains. It had my name written on it. I picked it up and tore it open, taking out a handwritten letter inside.

It began:

Dear Mr Preston,

I trust you will forgive us for what we have done as we hope so shall our maker. All our lifetime my wife and I have dutifully served three generations of the Loftbury family, but now in the twilight of our years can no longer continue with the new evil that is blighting our lives.

It was difficult for us to help the late Lord Loftbury dispose of the bodies of his wife, Margaret, and their dear children Henry and Felicity after he murdered them. It was an act that has ever since filled us with re-morse. But unyielding loyalty to the old family line has always been our code.

Now we have been drawn into the secrecy of our latest estate owner Lawrence Keating, and can no longer countenance being party to his illegal drug smuggling activities.

On the first night you were here, I alerted him on the false pretext of a fire breaking out in the garage at the back of the house. It is there that I shot him through the heart with an old service revolver, and then took his body in the Land Rover to bury him on the far side of the island. He was a bad man and I feel no guilt for that act.

Our regret is that we leave our wonderful son, David, and lovely dog Cannon behind. David is a mute, and though an adult, has the mental age of a child. He fre-quently wanders the island for days without returning home.

I have left this letter for you because my wife and I Laura believe you are a good man. Please do us the kindness of helping David find a place where his needs can be properly met. Your friend Lawrence would have discarded us. We have no other family and growing old it has become more and more difficult for us to care for David as we would have wished. Please find a good home for Cannon too.

Yours in gratitude and earnest,

Andrew McKellan

An age seemed to pass as I stood there taking in the gruesome details and pathos of the letter. So it was Andrew who had murdered and buried Lawrence and in a pact with his wife, I assumed, shot her and then himself in the head.

Completely bewildered and wondering what to do next, I became aware of a presence behind me. I turned. A man was standing in the open doorway. It was the mystery man I'd been chasing earlier. His hair tangled, mud and dirt streaked across his shirt and trousers. I realised this must be the couple's son, David.

He took a couple of steps inside staring at me, then caught sight of his parents' decaying bodies. His jaw dropped wide, abject disbelief rising on his face. The expression turned to anger, eyes narrowing in fury.

"I didn't do it!" I tried to explain, holding out the letter to him. That wasn't enough.

He leapt at me clutching my throat, sending me flying backwards. My head hit the floor and stunned me for a moment. His grip round my neck tightened and I began struggling for air as he pinned me down on my back laying on top of me. The grip was vice-like and I frantically rocked my body trying to roll him off me. Everything started growing hazy, my breath almost spent. With a last ditch attempt to survive I spat in his face.

He flinched for a second loosening his grip. It was enough to draw in a little air, at the same time swinging my right arm to punch him on the side of his head. He recoiled and this time I rolled him sideways on to the floor then sprung to my feet. David leapt up too, but in the brief pause I managed to draw the gun from my jacket pocket and raised it at him. He stopped.

God, I didn't want to shoot him. I was sick of all the killing. But it was me or him. In Andrew's letter he said his son had the mental age of a child. I could only hope my adversary would be able to gauge the danger pointing at him.

David backed away. Then turned and ran from the cottage. I followed him outside to see him sprinting down the track then veering off into a field to disappear from view behind a cluster of trees.

I left the cottage and closed the door. It didn't seem right that Andrew and Laura's bodies should be abandoned in their decaying, undignified repose, but right now I was in no mood to be their undertaker.

Grey cloud was beginning to sweep across the bay and I could feel spots of rain pinging my face. White surf was breaking on the waves agitated by a strong wind picking up. I didn't care how hard the rain might fall or how violent the wind would blow, I had no intention of sleeping in the mansion house that night.

Until someone arrived on the island so I could escape, my shelter would be the Land Rover. Although even that was now tainted by the thought of Lawrence's body being laid in it for burial by Andrew.

First I'd pack the possessions in my room to keep them in the vehicle, and then only enter the house for water and any food that hadn't gone off.

It was early evening and the thickening cloud added to the growing darkness. It seemed like a Dracula moment where I had to hurry and collect my things before the powers of the night consumed me inside the house.

With little light penetrating the reception hall windows, the place was already nearly dark. I could still see the stairway, but had the torch to pick out the detail. Every creak of the steps seemed to resonate eerily. As I collected my things in the room, I took great satisfaction in knowing I wouldn't have to suffer the leering gloat of the cherub anymore. Childishly I gave it two fingers.

Leaving the bedroom and walking along the corridor my eyes caught sight of a figure standing by the balcony. Lawrence! I dropped the travel bag in amazement.

He looked at me, smiling.

"You're not dead!" I shouted, totally stunned by his appearance.

He didn't reply, but turned and started ascending the stairs to the second floor balcony. I followed, annoyed that he'd just ignored me. What was he up to? The trickery and deceit of this man was beginning to deeply piss me off. Now he'd even faked his own death.

On the second floor he began walking down *that* passageway. The one containing the Loftbury's room and the spiral stairway at the end leading to the place where I'd seen Lord Loftbury entering to murder his family.

I faltered, wondering if I should go on. But I had to confront Lawrence. Now there was very little light to see clearly, just a vague shadow of him as he progressed along the corridor. I decided to follow, using the torch to see my way. He stopped outside the Loftbury bedroom, opened the door and entered.

With serious misgivings about going any further, it was only the desire to see Lawrence face to face, and demand to know what other tricks he'd played that drove me on.

I approached the door and slowly opened it. Entering, I shone the torch beam into the darkness of the room.

It picked out a man swinging by the neck from a rope knotted to the hook in the ceiling beam. The sheer horror of the sight hypnotised me. It was Lord Loftbury, his face contorted by the noose squeezing the life out of him.

Then the expression on his face changed. A broad smile raised the moustache on his upper lip as he stared at me. Next moment he broke into loud laughter, seeming to relish the terror he was inflicting on me.

Yet worse. In the next second he was no longer swinging on the rope, but standing on the floor free from its grasp. Now clasping a long handled axe in both hands, he began to raise it approaching me.

The torch fell from my grasp and I fled out of the room back along the corridor, stumbling in the dark and just barely able to see the shape of the stairway bannister as I grabbed it to guide me down. His cruel laughter echoed round the hall as I ran across to the door, guided by the faint twilight in the windows on each side.

The laughter grew louder and closer. I turned the door handle, but it was locked. In frenzied panic I pushed the door with all my might and began to shoulder it. It still wouldn't budge. Now I saw Loftbury descending the stairs, glowing in the dark, axe at the ready to swing.

Suddenly I remembered the door opened inward. In my terror I'd been trying to force it outwards. I threw it open and fled to the Land Rover parked on the forecourt outside. Leaping into the driver's seat, I glanced back at the house. Standing at the open door I saw Lawrence looking across at me. Then he vanished. The shock struck me. I hadn't been pursuing Lawrence through the house. I'd been following his ghost.

I switched on the headlights and accelerated hard away to the storehouse where I planned to spend the rest of the night. Pulling up outside, with the beam of the headlights lighting the building, I checked inside wondering if the mystery man I now knew to be David might be hiding in there. Except for the crates, the place was empty.

Among all the other revelations that had been sprung on me since I'd arrived on this ill-fated island, the fact that Andrew and Laura had a son here was another unexpected surprise and I wondered if Lawrence had been aware of the fact. Not that it mattered to him now.

The threatening grey cloud and rain had disappeared as quickly as it had come. The night sky was clear save for lumps of cloud that occasionally blotted out the moon. But there was enough light for me to see my way around after turning off the Land Rover headlights. Not that I intended to spend it in the open. I thought about resting overnight in the vehicle, but somehow the storehouse seemed more secure. Apart from the windows, it was built of solid brick.

Inside I bolted the door and aided by the presence of the gun felt a bit more secure against any unwelcome visitors, though neither would protect me from the intrusion of ghosts. I could only hope they were confined to the precincts of the house. Though they continued to haunt my mind.

The image of Lord Loftbury swinging in the noose and then his pursuit of me with the axe. Lawrence's dead body and his ghost. The screams of Lady Loftbury and her children being murdered. My worst nightmares in sleep couldn't compare to the horrific waking nightmare of this island. I wasn't sure how much longer I could maintain my sanity if I didn't escape from this accursed place soon.

For the second time in my stay at the storehouse, I climbed on to one of the unopened crates to lay down in great discomfort, but preferable to the concrete floor.

Sleep was impossible. Whenever I closed my eyes, bizarre images of my encounters swirled in an endless stream torturing my brain. An hour or so had passed when I heard a noise outside. My heart leapt into overdrive. I reached for the gun resting on the crate beside me.

The sound was like scratching on the stony ground outside the door. I slipped quietly off the crate and tip-toed to the window keeping close to the side. Then the night stillness was broken by a loud cry like high pitched barking.

I looked out the window. In the starry light I could see the shape of a dog. God. Was I now being haunted by the ghost of Cannon? Another apparition would be too much to bear. Then I realised it was a fox. The creature sniffed around at the ground then began barking several more times before wandering off into the darkness.

A wave of tremendous relief came over me. I laughed and then started to cry. It was like a safety valve bursting open. The simplicity of the creature was a sign that outside of my own harrowing world, nature and normal life was continuing as usual. That gave me hope.

The relief was brief. Memories of the horrors returned to haunt me. I wondered if Rosie was doing anything to try and find out why I hadn't returned. Surely she must be growing concerned? I sometimes changed my plans on a whim, but I'd always get in touch with her.

It seemed like an eternity before the dawn light began seeping through the window. Exactly what I'd do next to escape the island was unclear, but I decided to drive back to the bay in the hope someone would arrive in a launch to rescue me. Someone bringing food supplies perhaps, mail deliveries. I had no idea of arrangements for these things. Whether they were set by delivery to the island or collection from the mainland.

It was beginning to enter my head that I might try to construct a crude boat from materials in the garage at the back of the house. Boat building was not my forte, but something, anything that could help me to get away from here.

I drove back to the house and parked on the forecourt. The sun was starting to edge above the horizon across the bay in a clear blue sky. Waves lapped gently on the shore. Everything seemed calm, gulls gliding and swooping for catches in the waters below. This island could be heavenly if not for its dark secrets and ghoulish inhabitants.

I walked down the track to the jetty and looked out to sea. The mist that invariably masked the distance was absent, and I could clearly see the outline of the mainland. How I wished I could reach it. As I stared across the waves, I glimpsed what seemed to be an indistinct dot of something far away travelling on them. Maybe it was just a mirage created by the early morning light.

As I continued to watch, the dot began to grow larger. It was a launch! My spirits leapt for joy. Someone was coming. Joy suddenly turned to fear. What if it was Jack returning with Eddie to hunt me down?

I dreaded the prospect of taking cover in the house to see who was coming, but I had no intention of going on the run again unless it was absolutely necessary. And at least I now had a gun for protection. Reluctantly I decided to enter the house so my enemies couldn't pick me off easily in the open.

With misgivings I quickly made my way back up the track and entered the front door. The atmosphere of ghosts and murder lingered oppressively. From a window on the half landing between the first and second floors I could see down to the bay.

A few minutes later the yellow hulled launch with a white cabin pulled alongside the jetty. A man tied the boat to the capstans and then helped someone else off the vessel. It was a woman in a blue dress. They began walking towards the track leading up to the house. As I watched them approach, a huge surge of happiness flowed through every vein in my body. The woman was Rosie.

The sound of another engine broke the air. A few hundred yards out to sea a second launch was approaching the jetty.

I'd been about to run down the stairs to greet Rosie, but I saw she had stopped with the man beside her in green T-shirt and jeans to see who else was arriving at the island.

I was curious too. The red launch pulled in close to the other boat at the jetty and two men quickly disembarked. They walked up to Rosie and her companion and started talking to them as they all continued up the sloping track to the house.

My happiness at seeing Rosie collapsed. It was Jack who'd arrived in the second launch, alongside him was another heavily built henchman who I didn't recognise. It wasn't Eddie. My instinct was to get Rosie to safety. I had the gun, but any attempt to try and shoot Jack and his companion through the sealed window would be futile. The glass would shatter, but the bullets would fly off with hopeless inaccuracy. That would make the situation worse.

As I desperately began calculating a better plan, I caught sight of a figure running out from the side of the house. It was David. Unseen by the arrivals who were still on the lower level of the track, he took cover on the right side of the Land Rover.

Now I was in total confusion. What was he doing by complicating matters even more?

As Rosie and the others reached the top of the slope on to the forecourt, the big man with Jack grabbed hold of Rosie's arm. She tried to pull away at the same moment as Jack produced a gun and pointed it at the man in the green T-shirt, waving the weapon to make him continue walking.

The heavy tugged Rosie along as they all began passing the Land Rover. My anger was at bursting point. Just before I turned to sprint down the stairway, my eye caught sight of David leaping out from behind the vehicle and flinging himself furiously at the bastard forcing Rosie on.

Huge though he was, the heavy lost his balance and fell hurtling to the ground releasing his grip on Rosie. David started beating him in a frenzy.

I flew down the stairs reaching the front door which was half open. Throwing it back I saw Jack pointing his gun to try and pick out David as he rolled on the ground with his giant opponent.

Rosie and her companion were starting to run for cover at the side of the house. Jack raised his gun to take aim at them.

"Jack!" I shouted, stepping out of the doorway. Like lightning he swung round. I fired a shot at him. He staggered back, but still standing loosed a shot at me. I heard the crack in the same second feeling a sharp pain in my stomach. My legs felt weak, about to give way.

I fired at him again. He staggered back further, attempting to strike another shot. The gun waved erratically. He stumbled to keep his balance before collapsing on to the ground.

My head was starting to spin. I caught sight of what I thought was David getting up from the ground with the big man laying still. Rosie and her companion were running towards me. I seemed to be moving backwards through the door opening into the house. I heard her screaming 'get on the radio!"

For a moment I appeared to be nowhere, in some sort of spinning limitless void. Then I was standing up inside the hall feeling absolutely fine.

Rosie was kneeling beside someone laying on their back in the hall.

"Hang on! Please hang on! Help is coming." she cried.

I couldn't work why she seemed so upset.

"What's the matter?" I called to her. I was standing beside her, but she didn't seem to hear. Then I saw who was on the floor.

Me!

Blood had entirely soaked my shirt and was spreading in a pool on the floor. Next moment my eyes caught sight of some figures a short distance away at the foot of the hall stairs.

Lord Loftbury stood there, that scheming grin on his lips, a triumphant gleam in his eyes. Beside him was his wife, Lady Margaret Loftbury and on each side of them their two children Henry and Felicity. Andrew and Laura stood nearby. Lawrence was descending the stairs to join them.

"I see we have a new resident in the house," Lord Loftbury announced, smiling smugly. "Andrew and Laura will be serving dinner at eight o'clock. You are welcome to join us in the dining room," he formally invited me.

The horrifying revelation struck. I was dead! Jack's bullet had dealt me a fatal blow. I was now condemned to be a restless spirit residing with these spectres in the house of hell.

They began to approach me. At that moment I saw the man who'd come with Rosie entering the doorway and kneeling beside her to attend my lifeless body.

The setting began to grow hazy. Distant. Everything starting to disappear. I felt myself floating in another immense void. Urgent voices echoed in the swirling chasm of my mind. They made no sense other than a vague awareness of orders, instructions. I felt sick. Nausea coursed through me.

CHAPTER 8

IT felt as though I'd been away forever when my eyes flicked open. I had no idea where I was. A light shone down on me from a white ceiling as I stared upwards laying on my back.

My eyes caught sight of a stand on my left. Clear fluid in plastic bags hanging on it with tubes leading into my arm.

A woman was standing on the other side smiling. I had a notion that I knew her from somewhere, but couldn't place it. The woman seemed excited.

"Nurse! Nurse!" she called. "He's come round!"

The woman turned back to me.

"I'm Rosie," she said, a beautiful smile rising again on her face. I tried to return a smile.

****

A large tent had been erected in a field on Fennamore island. Inside a group of people wearing white, forensic suits and masks carefully lifted Lawrence's decomposing body on to a stretcher.

Outside the tent an area of the field's topsoil had been removed and another forensic team was spread out carefully scraping the surface, delving into the soil below.

"Over here," one of them called. "I think I've found something."

Back at the mansion house, yet more searching was taking place. Every inch of every room painstakingly being examined. When several plastic bags containing white powder were found under the floorboards in one of them, the house was temporarily evacuated until proper filtration breathing masks arrived.

One of the bags discovered had split open and particles of the powder were likely to be circulating in the house.

Police helicopters became a frequent sight arriving and departing from the island. The media had been excluded, but that didn't stop the buzz of publicity generated by the growing rumours of grisly finds on the otherwise peaceful island. Speculation and legend rose to fantastic heights in the absence of fact.

****

It was several weeks before I was finally released from hospital. For the first couple of days I had no recollection of what had happened to me, except I was recovering from a bullet wound where the projectile had entered just below my heart. It was a miracle that I'd survived.

That was down to Rosie and, in particular, the boatman she'd hired to take her to the island when she'd grown anxious about me not returning home. Thankfully he was also an experienced first aider and had managed to stem the flow of blood from my body and resuscitate my heart before the air ambulance arrived. Thankfully too, he had a radio on board the boat to alert the coastguard. Otherwise I would have had no chance of surviving for long after the boatman brought me back from the dead.

The memory of events on the island gradually crept back. Memories that I wished could forever be erased from my mind.

Rosie was my strength and rock. She moved into my London flat and nursed me for a few weeks while I was too weak to move much. Depression dragged me down and despite my bouts of rudeness and anger at the most trivial things, she resolutely stayed by my side.

Not long after I returned home the phone calls started. Press and TV media harassing for interviews about events on the island. Again Rosie was my guardian fending them off. At one point we seriously thought of going into hiding, but when the police called round to see me one day, the option of disappearing for a while came to an end. I'd become a person of interest to them.

Their visit was a shock.

Two grim looking officers in grey suits arrived and placed me under arrest for the killing of William Mason, who I learned was the real name of the hoodlum I knew as Jack. They questioned me on what had happened. I told them of Lawrence's drug running activities, of finding his partially buried body, and the corpses of Andrew and Laura. My confrontation with Jack, or William Mason, was totally in self-defence I insisted.

At the stories of my hauntings, the officers glanced at each other, obviously disbelieving me, but took note of it in my statement.

Because of my medical condition I didn't have to go to the police station, but the following day another officer called to take my fingerprints and DNA sample. I felt like I was the criminal instead of the scum I'd eliminated.

Now it could be months before a decision was taken to charge me with his killing or not. But a lot can happen in that time.

The first was sharp knocking at the door and repeated ringing of the doorbell one evening a few days later. A heavily built, dark suited man wearing a sour expression greeted me.

"Detective Inspector Roy Hodge, Metropolitan Police, I have a warrant to search this place," he announced, thrusting the document almost into my face. At that he barged past me followed by four other police officers hurrying into the flat.

Rosie had just finished taking a shower. She appeared in her dressing gown wondering what was happening.

The officers swarmed through the flat, turning out the contents of drawers, cupboards, lifting rugs, throwing back the bedsheets, up-ending the mattress, generally delving into every nook and cranny of the place.

"Why are doing this?" Rosie shouted, deeply upset. "This man is recovering from a serious injury. You can't do this to him."

Her protest went unheeded. After half-an-hour, and appearing not to find what they were seeking, the officers left without a word of apology. The flat couldn't have looked any worse than if thieves had turned the place over.

"Right!" Rosie was furious. "We're not going to put up with this. I have a friend who knows a brilliant criminal lawyer. Whatever nonsense the police are trying to stick on you, we're going to fight it with the best."

We had already consulted a solicitor to appoint a criminal defence lawyer. But Rosie felt hers would be a better choice. It was becoming obvious the powers that be were gunning for me. After all the horror of the island, I was now facing a new horror on my doorstep.

True to her word, a few days later the lawyer she found through her friend called at the flat. He looked to be in his late forties with bright eyes, wisps of grey in his brown hair and a welcoming handshake.

"This is Gareth Edwards," Rosie introduced him.

We settled with coffee in the living room, where I related all that had happened. He asked me some questions then promised to consider my position and get back to me.

Another couple of weeks passed. I remained in a state of purgatory limbo not knowing what was going to happen, with the possibility of facing a trial where I'd unjustly be sent to prison for killing a vile specimen of humanity.

I began to wonder if I should contact a newspaper and sell my story. If I was going down, at least I'd probably make good money to have on my release. Something in return for all the misery I'd suffered.

In the event things started to take a different turn a week later.

For the first time since I'd returned home from hospital, I made a short trip into the world outside to a Chinese restaurant near my flat in Fulham. Walking hand in hand with Rosie, the early evening sights and sounds of the street seemed strangely uplifting, after being trapped on that dreadful island and then confined at home for so long.

Halfway through our meal Rosie's phone rang. She looked attentive listening to the caller.

"It's Gareth Edwards, the lawyer," she said ending the call. "He says he has some information and is it okay to pop round? I told him it was."

It was disappointing we'd have to cut short our evening out, but we were intrigued to know what he had to tell us.

Gareth arrived soon after we returned, and taking up my offer of a glass of wine, we settled with our drinks in the living room.

"Among the many contacts in my work," he began, "I know a senior police officer who has some insight into your case."

He paused, taking a sip of wine.

"Of course, anything I tell you now is in the strictest confidence." He looked at us for confirmation. We agreed his terms.

"You told the police how you discovered Lawrence was drug dealing on the island, but it seems the police suspect you were involved in the business too."

Gareth's revelation shocked me. I was speechless for a moment. He leaned forward, searching me with his eyes.

"If I'm to defend you in this criminal case, I have to ask, did you have any involvement in this drug running network?"

"None at all!" I was furious that I'd been connected in this way. Now I realised why the police had searched my flat. They were looking for a drugs stash, some evidence to connect me with Lawrence's network.

"This is ridiculous!" I stood up and a sharp pain seared across my stomach. Rosie took my shoulder, urging me to calm down.

"Why would they think I'm involved?" I sat down again trying to relax a little.

"Well, in the forensic search of the house, they found a stash of cocaine in powder form under the floorboards of a room," he explained. "It's a very potent, new deviant of the drug that has powerful hallucinogenic properties. Like a new sort of LSD. One of the bags was split open and that room had your fingerprints all over it." Gareth paused again.

"Did that room have a marble cherub figure attached to the wall?" I asked.

"I believe my contact did say there was some sort of marble figurine in the room," Gareth replied.

"Well that's the room I stayed in. Of course it would have my fingerprints all over it."

"They also found your prints in a storehouse on the island containing crates with the same drug in tablet form," Gareth continued.

"But I took refuge in there. I told you." I began to panic thinking as well as facing a killing charge, I was now being set up as a drug dealer."

"It's okay. Calm down. This is all very circumstantial and I'm sure the police won't have anything to connect you with drug running," Gareth attempted to reassure me.

"Can't they track down the real criminals involved?" Rosie broke in.

Gareth took another sip of wine. I downed the rest of mine.

"The police have made arrests of gangland members in London and Glasgow in Scotland. And I believe arrests are imminent in America," Gareth explained. "The drug manufacturing base hidden in that remote Scottish highland cottage is deserted though. Whoever was involved there in refining the cocaine into a powerful deviant of the drug has fled."

He paused again for a moment before continuing.

"That was Lawrence's problem I think. He was suddenly left with not being able to receive sufficient refined supplies to ship to his connections. The person or persons at the cottage must have got wind of some undercover operation closing in and just disappeared."

It seemed ironic to me that it wasn't any mobsters who killed Lawrence, but his servant Andrew who had no links with the criminal underworld. Which brought me back to my own predicament.

"Can you tell me if I have any chance of not being convicted for killing this Jack criminal bastard, or whatever his real name is?"

Gareth's expression grew serious.

"Well you admitted to shooting him in self-defence and a jury might accept that. But it all depends if the prosecution service decides whether there's enough evidence to bring a murder or manslaughter charge that would be likely to convict you."

It was not the news I wanted to hear, but not a surprise. Before leaving Gareth promised to keep in regular contact.

Another week passed where I fought hard not to sink into a pit of depression again. Rosie encouraged me to see a film with her and go to a theatre show. Also for walks in a nearby park, which helped to keep my spirits up.

Then one evening as we were about to eat dinner a news item on the TV grabbed our attention.

Police have confirmed that the decomposed bodies of a woman and two children found on the Scottish island of Fennamore, are that of Lady Margaret Loftbury and her son and daughter Henry and Felicity. The bodies were found in a field near to where the body of Lawrence Keating, the late owner of the island, was recently unearthed.

Lady Loftbury was reported to have left her husband, Lord Ernest Loftbury, two years ago taking the children with her to Canada. No-one had been able to contact them since. A year ago Lord Loftbury took his own life at the family home on Fennamore island.

The island was also the scene of the recent killing of alleged gangland member William Mason, and the bodies of elderly husband and wife, Andrew and Laura McKellan were recently found on the island. Police are still investigating a major drugs haul uncovered there.

I turned off the TV. The horror of the place was flooding back. So it was true as recorded in Andrew's suicide letter. He had helped bury the murdered bodies of his master's wife and children. Returning memories of the island sickened me.

Rosie could see my distress and suggested going out for a while. But now I had no desire for the meal we'd prepared or for going anywhere. I drank a couple of glasses of wine and then went to bed, the night filled with restless dreams and visions of all the terror I'd suffered on that cursed island.

A few days later Rosie and I were out shopping in the local supermarket when the phone rang. It was Gareth. She was listening to him intently, a serious expression on her face. I braced myself for some grim news. The call ended.

"It's over," she said, a blank expression on her face.

"What's over?" I was totally bemused. A woman standing nearby in the supermarket turned to look at us. A smile started to rise on Rosie's face.

"Gareth says the prosecution service has decided there isn't enough evidence to get a successful conviction against you."

I stood there stunned.

"He's learnt that the boatman who brought me over to the island, and helped to save your life, has given an independent witness statement," Rosie explained. "He says he would testify in court that you shot that bastard in self-defence. The boatman's word would carry more weight than mine, given our relationship, and a jury would probably take your side."

Rosie hugged me. The woman nearby said 'well done', though she obviously had no idea what we were on about.

I felt ecstatic. Then realised in the tension that I'd crushed the box of cereal I was holding.

"But the drugs. I could still have that stuck on me," my joy sank.

"No. The whole lot is dropped. You're free," Rosie confirmed.

The relief that came over me was more than I could bear at that moment. I began to feel moisture welling in my eyes, and not wishing to make a fool of myself in the supermarket, stepped outside into the fresh air while Rosie took over the rest of the shopping. She was my true gem in so many ways.

For some time there had been a thought lingering in the back of my mind. Something that Gareth had said about the forensic search in the mansion house. The consignment of hallucinogenic drug that had been stored in powder form beneath the floorboards in my room on the island.

Had some of the powder in the split bag escaped through the boards so that I was inhaling it? Had I begun to hallucinate in seeing the spectres? Caused me to believe that the cherub had some supernatural power? And Rosie seeing Lady Loftbury standing beside the bed. Was that a drugged illusion?

But gangster Eddie had been spooked by seeing a ghostly woman. He hadn't been in my room. And when I briefly died, and saw the ghosts in my out of body experience. My invitation to join Lord Loftbury and the other spirits for dinner. I hadn't been in the room just before that. Surely I wasn't hallucinating then?

Maybe I'd never know for sure. But the thought of spending eternity as a resident ghost in that house really would have been a fate worse than death.

During the next few weeks I tried to contact various social service agencies in Scotland to see if I could track down what had happened to David. But not being a relative, I wasn't allowed information on his whereabouts.

I could only hope that he was being cared for properly. And I would like to have thanked him for saving Rosie from the clutches of that henchman who came to the island with Jack.

At least I was able to ring and thank the boatman in Scotland who helped save my life and was prepared to act as a witness to my innocence in Jack's killing.

As for Rosie and me, we sold our flats and pooled our money to buy an apartment together in Chelsea, not far from where we'd already been living. We talked of marriage, but that was something we'd eventually get round to.

****

It was a year later when a story in the newspaper grabbed my attention. The article said a leisure group company had bought the mansion house on Fennamore island and was converting the property and surrounding area into a centre for sporting activities.

Workmen clearing the house were hoisting the figure of a marble cherub through a first floor window when the hoist cable snapped. The cherub crashed to the ground, crushing one of the workmen beneath to death.

Work was stopped on the house for several days. When it resumed, some of the workers reported unusual events inside the property, claiming they'd seen ghosts. A halt was called to the whole refurbishment project.

It confirmed to me I hadn't been hallucinating. That the marble cherub was contaminated with evil, and the hauntings had all been real on my deadly island retreat.

I hope you enjoyed *Deadly Island Retreat*. If you would like to read more of my books they are listed below and available through Amazon.

As a taster, I include here the first part of my popular novel:

THE BEATRICE CURSE

THE CURSE BEGINS

October 10th 1763

TWO SINISTER men in black hooded robes gripped the arms of a woman, dragging her towards a large wooden stake driven deep into the soil of a grassy meadow.

The breeze ruffled the woman's long black dress and swept knotted, dark hair across her sallow, sunken face as she mouthed obscenities into the air.

Roughly her captors shoved her back against the stake and tied her hands and feet behind with ropes.

Four more robed men joined them, stacking brushwood around the woman. The surrounding crowd of villagers were electrified by the scene shouting 'BURN THE

WITCH!... SEND HER TO HELL!... ROAST HER ALIVE!'

The spectators pelted the staked prisoner with stones and rotten vegetables, as the hooded men piled the brushwood higher. They left for a moment, returning shortly carrying blazing pine resin torches, flickering in the shadowy twilight.

A roar of delight rose from the crowd as the men stooped with the torches to light the brushwood around the stake and its victim.

The woman continued to mouth obscenities, and some heard a terrible curse rise from her lips as the brushwood flames sprang upwards, at first licking at her bare feet, then catching on to her dress and erupting in fury.

The curses turned into cries of pain and as the heat began to fry her flesh, the cries turned to pitiful, agonising screams, the conflagration consuming all in its path to leave a mass of charcoal.

Ecstatic at the spectacle, the villagers began slowly returning to their homes as the flames gradually died away. They were relieved the witch was gone. Consigned to hell. They were safe once more.

CHAPTER 1

THE HORROR of the Beatrice Curse came to haunt me two hundred years after the witch burned at the stake.

I was a young man in the amazing days of the 1960s. A time when my world was filled with supreme confidence and belief of great things to come.

Even now, in the later years of my life, the horror of what really happened grows vivid again, as I record the terrifying events that changed everything. Events that nearly ended my life and caused me to kill. But I'm compelled to record the story, to warn a future generation.

My ambition back then was to carve out a career as an author.

Of course, the chances of succeeding were slim with so many great writers whose books exceeded my novice skills. However, I was convinced my name, Mark Roberts, would one day rate among their glorious ranks.

I'd gained good degrees in English and History at university. My father hoped I'd join the family furniture business which he'd set up as a young man in London.

But I wanted something more exciting than that. We argued. In the end he agreed he would grant me money to finance a month long stay at Deersmoor, a remote west country village in the county of Devon.

It was intended I would write my novel there and, if I succeeded in finding a top publisher, he'd happily let me follow my star. If not, I'd join the family firm.

My hope was to write in peace and tranquillity in the beautiful countryside surroundings. In reality I'd taken a step into hell.

A cab took me on the five mile journey from the train station to the village. As it travelled along the high street past the local shops, I felt I'd been transported back in time.

Everything looked so quaint. White thatched cottages and shop fronts with brown and dark green liveries declaring their businesses, butcher, baker, greengrocer and all. Nothing like the bright and colourful window displays that dazzled in west London where I lived, with the swinging 1960s bursting into life.

The cottage I rented was just a short distance from the high street, tucked along a narrow lane with a woodland opposite. It was fairly basic with a small kitchen, living room and two upstairs bedrooms, but looked ideal for providing the peace I desired.

The first week was perfect. I spent time sketching out plots for my novel and walked to the high street to pick up provisions. The world seemed as it should be.

Then came the change.

Late one afternoon I heard a loud rapping on the front door. A beautiful young woman stood there. For a second I could have been back home. She wore a cream top and dark red miniskirt with a brass buckle belt circling her slim frame. Coupled with her pixie crop chestnut hair, the style was fashionable sixties London.

She greeted me with a mixture of smile and concern.

"I'm so sorry to disturb you, but my grandmother is dying. She wants to see you," my visitor pleaded.

"Me? Why me?"

"She's heard you're a writer and wants to tell you something."

I was baffled. What could she want to tell me? A complete stranger. I agreed to come and grabbed my denim jacket.

"It's only a short walk," she said. "Just behind the high street."

As I walked beside her I introduced myself.

"I know your name," she replied. I was surprised.

"News travels fast here. No secrets," she smiled. "I'm Alison Carpenter."

She asked if I was enjoying my stay in the village and seemed puzzled that I'd want to come to this 'backwater' place, as she put it, from a city like London.

Soon we were in a street of white terraced houses and halfway down stopped at a dark blue door. Alison knocked and an older woman opened it. She peered at me suspiciously.

"This is Mark Roberts, the writer," Alison introduced us. "And this is my mother, Emma."

Her mother stepped aside to let us in. I sensed from her I wasn't welcome.

"My grandmother's in here," Alison led me to a door down the hallway. Inside an elderly woman with a drawn and colourless face, almost skeletal, stared blankly towards the ceiling from her bed.

A well dressed man in a dark suit stood nearby.

"This is Doctor Newton. He says grandmother doesn't have long to live," Alison introduced us in a whisper. The doctor nodded a greeting.

She led me to the bedside. The old woman's eyes shifted slightly to gaze at me.

"This is the writer granny," said Alison.

The old woman began to say something. I knelt down to hear her.

"Beatrice is rising again. You must stop her," she spoke in a weak, breathless voice, but the tone of concern was unmistakable. "Write about it. Tell the world. She must be stopped. I didn't start the fire."

"Who's Beatrice? What fire?" I asked.

The grandmother was exhausted. She tried to reply, but the words wouldn't come.

"That's enough," Alison's mother Emma stepped forward. "Leave her be."

Next moment the bedroom door opened.

A young woman in a red lace blouse and white miniskirt entered, her fair hair styled in a beehive.

"I got the message to come," she sounded alarmed.

"Grandma!" She rushed to the bedside kneeling and taking hold of the dying woman's hand. Her grandmother remained motionless.

"Oh God! I think she's gone."

Alison and her mother crossed to the bed. I felt like an intruder on a deeply personal moment.

The doctor examined the old lady and announced that she'd passed away.

The women began crying. The moment was too intimate for me to remain. I whispered to the doctor I was leaving.

"It's best for now," he replied.

As I walked back to the cottage, my head was spinning with the events. The mysterious message about someone called Beatrice. That she must be stopped. And suddenly being thrust into the deathbed scene of complete strangers.

What I was meant to do to stop this Beatrice from rising made no sense. Write what about her? Stop her from doing what? Little did I know how Beatrice would become the greatest danger of my life.

Back at the cottage I settled down to writing my novel again, but the strange business at the house kept interrupting my thoughts.

An hour later came another knock at the door. I opened it. Alison had returned.

"I'm sorry about all that," she began. "I didn't mean to embarrass you. That was my sister, Barbara, who came in. I couldn't introduce you at that moment."

"It's okay. Don't worry. I thought it best to leave. Come inside."

"No, I've got to get back," Alison declined.

"I didn't understand what your grandmother was saying. She said something about stopping Beatrice rising again. I've no idea what she meant," I explained.

"Beatrice was reputed to be a witch. She was burned at the stake two hundred years ago. It's an old legend in the village," said Alison.

Now I was even more mystified.

"Don't worry about it. My grandmother was very old and her mind was wandering a lot."

With that explanation I thought all was now laid to rest.

"I came to say my gran's funeral is on Wednesday next week. We're holding a wake after the service and I thought you could come along and meet some of our friends in the village."

I was doubtful.

"I know it's not a happy occasion, but gran was ill for some time and her death was not unexpected. I'm sure she'd have been pleased to welcome you to the village."

Alison's beautiful, pleading hazel eyes captured me. I was enchanted and helpless.

"Okay. If you would like," I conceded.

"At my house, three-thirty on Wednesday." She smiled then turned and left.

Over the next few days I settled to working on my novel again. When Wednesday afternoon arrived I set off for Alison's house. I hadn't been prepared for attending a sombre occasion during my stay and could only find a black donkey jacket coupled with black jeans by way of respect.

The chatter of family and friends flowed from inside as Alison opened the front door. She wore a black dress suit and looked absolutely radiant despite the nature of the occasion. For a moment all eyes turned towards me when I entered the crowded living room, making me feel extremely self-conscious.

"So pleased you could come," said Alison. "Have some wine." She reached for a glass on a table covered with drinks and light spreads.

As I took the glass, a bearded man with curly ginger hair approached. He was dressed in a brown corduroy jacket and trousers and peered at me through dark, horn rimmed spectacles. He had the appearance of a literary or artistic person. Maybe a college lecturer.

"Is this our new resident writer?" he posed the question to Alison while staring at me.

Alison introduced us.

"Mark, meet Rupert Long. He owns our local bookshop in the high street. I'm sure you'll have a lot in common on the subject of books and authors."

We shook hands.

"Just a novice beginner," I told him modestly.

"Well, even the greats were novices once upon a time," he said encouragingly.

"So how did you get to know Alison and the family?" Rupert enquired.

Alison interrupted.

"Granny asked to see him on her deathbed. She was mumbling something about Beatrice rising again. Her mind was wandering a bit."

"Ah, Beatrice the witch. The curse." Rupert broke in. "Of course, it's the 200th anniversary of her burning at the stake in 1763."

"What's this about Beatrice?" A woman who I recognised as Alison's sister, Barbara, entered the conversation. She wore a long-sleeved black dress and her fair hair was no longer in a beehive, but spread around her shoulders. Her face was slightly harder, more businesslike than the softer features of her sister, though the woman's engaging eyes shared the same family root.

"We're just talking about grandma's last words with Mark," Alison explained.

"We haven't been properly introduced. I'm Barbara," she turned to me and shook my hand. "And this is my fiancée Malcolm Rushton."

I nodded a greeting. Malcolm was well groomed, brown short hair with a smile that looked a bit oily.

The gathering began to grow as another man joined us. A tough, sinewy face and probably in his mid-forties with a gaze that seemed to be constantly searching our every movement.

"This is police sergeant Robert Fellows, our local law and order," Alison introduced us.

"Bob please. Call me Bob. I'm not on duty now," his strict features rose to a smile.

"I hear you're a writer," the officer turned his searching gaze on me. "Not a lot happens in this village," he said.

"Only behind closed doors," Barbara joked.

The group laughed. I felt completely outside the loop among people who obviously knew each other well.

"We were talking about Alison and Barbara's grandmother," Rupert the bookshop man brought the conversation back to its earlier direction. "She told Mark about the Beatrice curse."

"I've no idea what she meant," I said.

"Well if you're interested, come to my bookshop tomorrow and I'll tell you all about it," Rupert invited me.

"What's all this about Beatrice?" The sisters' mother Emma joined us. She wore a black dress suit. Her stern face matched the darkness of her outfit.

"Rupert was telling Mark about the witch," Alison explained.

"I don't think we should be talking about all that at your grandmother's funeral reception," she said disapprovingly.

"My mother was very old, muddled in her thinking. I've no idea why she should start going on about Beatrice. She was burned at the stake 200 years ago."

"Well we burn her effigy on a bonfire every year at the Burning Beatrice festival," said Alison. "Maybe in her confused state granny thought it was all real."

"She said Beatrice was rising again," I interrupted.

Emma glared at me, an unwelcome intruder on personal family affairs. Her eyes conveyed resentment at my presence. I sensed her hostility also masked an inner fear. The group fell into an embarrassed silence. I wished the floor would open up and swallow me.

"Come over here and meet some of my other friends," Alison came to the rescue and led me across to another group of people chatting.

I spent the next hour in small talk and answering questions on why I'd come to the village. Local gossip and rumours seemed to have built me into a famous author staying in their midst, instead of my true status as a rank amateur. But it felt good, if undeserved.

At the reception, I noticed a man dressed even less formally than me for the occasion in red T-shirt and blue jeans. He was strongly built and had long, straggly brown hair. His unshaven face looked permanently brooding, as if ready to attack anyone who gave him the slightest offence.

Alison noticed me occasionally glancing at him while he stood alone throughout the gathering.

"That's our cousin, Josh Williams," she answered my unspoken curiosity. "A man who keeps himself very much to himself."

As she spoke I saw him look across at us. Quickly I averted my gaze fearing he might take offence at me staring.

"He's the woodkeeper of Fellswold, two hundred acres of local woodland," Alison explained. "It borders the road across from the cottage where you're staying. Come and meet him."

I didn't particularly want an introduction, but Alison led me over to the man. I held out my hand. He grudgingly reached out and shook mine in a painful grip of iron, the sullen look on his face unchanged as if I didn't exist.

"Mark's a writer. He's staying in the village for a while," Alison attempted to lighten the air.

"I know," the man replied in a voice of disinterest. He turned and left the room.

"He doesn't say much," Alison smiled. "But he must have liked you a teeny-weeny little bit, or else he wouldn't even have shook your hand."

I was massaging my hand, which felt like it had just been removed from a metal bench clamp.

When I left the gathering, a great sense of relief came over me. Apart from Josh the woodkeeper, and the sisters' mother Emma, they were a friendly bunch. But my feeling of being an outsider remained.

Back at the cottage I wasn't in the mood for writing and made a quick ham and cheese sandwich. There was no radio or television in the cottage, so I sat on the settee in the living room drinking coffee with some lustful thoughts about Alison. I wondered if I should ask her out for a meal one night. But she probably wasn't that interested in me. Just wanting to make me feel welcome.

The memory of her grandmother came back. The woman's deathbed rambling about Beatrice the witch. And the look of fear in the eyes of Alison's mother Emma, when I recalled the dying woman's words "Beatrice is rising again."

Rupert the bookshop owner had invited me to visit him if I wanted to know more about this enigmatic Beatrice. I decided to go to his book store tomorrow.

As Mark learns more, he finds himself gradually becoming entangled in Beatrice's evil clutches.

Find out what happens next in THE BEATRICE CURSE by Geoffrey Sleight.

Available on Amazon

The sequel BEATRICE CURSE II is also now available.

MORE BOOKS BY THE AUTHOR

DARK SECRETS COTTAGE

Shocking family secrets unearthed in a haunted cottage.

THE SOUL SCREAMS MURDER

Murderous trail of horror in a haunted house.

A GHOST TO WATCH OVER ME

A ghostly encounter exposes deadly revelations.

VENGEANCE ALWAYS DELIVERS

When a stranger calls – revenge strikes in a gift of riches.

THE ANARCHY SCROLL

Perilous fantasy adventure in a mysterious lost land.

All available on Amazon

For more information or if you have any questions
please email me:
geoffsleight@gmail.com

Or visit my Amazon Author page:
http://amazon.com/author/geoffreysleight

Tweet: http://twitter.com/resteasily

Your views and comments are welcome and appreciated.

Printed in Great Britain
by Amazon

24763264R00076